"It's not charity I'm offering.
It's a deal."

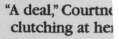

"A deal," Courtne... clutching at her...

Not love…

A deal…

"I will clear your debts if you do something for me in return."

"For heaven's sake, what?" It had to be something huge in return for three million dollars.

Jack looked worried for a second. "This might be a bit of a shock, coming so quickly after we've met. But I'm quite sure on my part. In fact, I've never been more sure of anything."

"Jack, for pity's sake, what?"

"I want you to have my child."

Some of our bestselling authors are Australians!

Lindsay Armstrong...
Helen Bianchin...
Emma Darcy...
Miranda Lee...

Look out for their novels about the
Wonder of Down Under—
where spirited women win the hearts of
Australia's most eligible men.

Coming soon:

A Question of Marriage
by Lindsay Armstrong
Harlequin Presents® #2208

He's big, he's brash, he's brazen...he's Australian!

Miranda Lee

MARRIAGE AT A PRICE

THE AUSTRALIANS

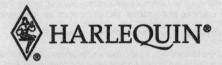

HARLEQUIN®

TORONTO • NEW YORK • LONDON
AMSTERDAM • PARIS • SYDNEY • HAMBURG
STOCKHOLM • ATHENS • TOKYO • MILAN • MADRID
PRAGUE • WARSAW • BUDAPEST • AUCKLAND

ISBN 0-373-12181-4

MARRIAGE AT A PRICE

First North American Publication 2001.

Copyright © 2001 by Miranda Lee.

Visit us at www.eHarlequin.com

Printed in U.S.A.

CHAPTER ONE

COURTNEY knew, the moment she saw William Sinclair's face, that her mother's accountant had *really* bad news. He'd hedged over the phone when she'd asked him if Crosswinds was in financial trouble, saying he just needed to have a little chat with her, face to face.

Courtney hadn't been fooled by that. Her mother's cost-cutting measures these past couple of years had been obvious to everyone. Staff was down to a minimum. The fences had not been painted. Other repairs had been left undone. The place had begun to look shabby. Which wasn't exactly good for business.

If Crosswinds was to compete against the lavish and very modern thoroughbred studs now gracing the Upper Hunter Valley, then it needed to look its very best.

When she'd pointed this out to her mother earlier in the year, Hilary hadn't agreed. 'What we need, daughter, is a new stallion. Not fancy stables.'

Which was also true. Four years earlier, when the stud had been doing very well, her mother had imported a classy Irish stayer named Four-Leaf Clover.

Unfortunately, the horse had contracted a virus and had died shortly after standing his first season at stud. His only crop of foals hadn't been much to look at as yearlings, bringing such poor bidding at auction that Hilary had stubbornly kept most of them rather than let them go for less than they'd cost to breed.

With Four-Leaf Clover gone, and their remaining two sires both getting older, Crosswinds had a real hole in its breeding program. But there hadn't been the money to buy a replacement till this year.

'I'll still have to look for a bargain,' her mother had told her. 'I haven't got much spare cash.'

Her mum had been cock-a-hoop when she'd arrived home with Goldplated in May, especially with the price she'd negotiated. Though no price was a real bargain, Courtney realised ruefully as she walked into the accountant's office, if the money to buy the darned horse had been borrowed.

William Sinclair rose as she entered, being the old-fashioned gentleman that he was. 'Good morning, Courtney,' he greeted. 'Do sit down.' And he waved her to the single chair facing his large, but *large*, ancient desk.

Courtney took off her Akubra hat and sat down, making herself as comfortable as she could in the stiff-backed seat. A fruitless exercise. Tension had already knotted the muscles between her shoulder blades.

The accountant dropped his eyes to the papers in front of him, then started shuffling them around.

Courtney's agitation rose. She wasn't in the mood for any further procrastination.

'Just give it to me straight, Bill,' she began bluntly, and his eyes lifted, his expression faintly disapproving. He'd never liked her calling him Bill. But that was rather irrelevant at the moment. 'No bulldust now. No waffle. I'm my mother's daughter. I can take it.'

William shook his head at the young woman sitting before him. Yes, she was indeed her mother's daughter, he thought wearily.

Not in looks. Lord, no. Hilary Cross had been as plain as a pikestaff. Her daughter had clearly taken after her father, that unknown, unspoken-of male who had miraculously impregnated the forty-five-year-old spinster owner of Crosswinds over a quarter of a century ago, then disappeared off the face of the earth.

Gossip claimed he'd been a gypsy, and Courtney's looks seemed to confirm that, with her long black curly hair, dark brown eyes and rich olive skin. A striking-looking girl, in William's opinion.

Her personality and ways, however, were pure Hilary. Just look at the way she was sitting, for heaven's sake, with her right ankle hooked up over her left knee. That was how *men* sat, not young ladies. And then there was the matter of her dress, 'dress' being the pertinent word. Because she never wore one! William had never seen her in anything but blue jeans and a checked shirt. Yet she had a very good figure.

As for that glorious hair of hers. It was always bundled up into a rough pony-tail, then shoved under a dusty brown stockman's hat. Lipstick never graced her deliciously full mouth. And the only scent he ever smelt on her was leather and horses!

But it was her manner that rankled William the most. Not quite as aggressive and opinionated as her mother, she was still far too tactless with people. And bold in her attitude all round. Bold as brass!

Of course, it wasn't her fault. Hilary had raised Courtney as though she were a boy, letting her run wild from the time she was a tiny tot. He could still remember the day he'd driven out to Crosswinds, when Courtney had been about eleven or twelve. She'd met him at the gate, riding a big black colt with a crazed look in its eye and wide, snorting nostrils. Far too much horse for a man, let alone a wisp of a girl.

'Race you up to the house,' she'd shouted from where the horse had been dancing around in circles, obviously eager to get going. 'Last one there is a rotten egg!' And, nudging the huge beast in the flanks with her heels, she'd taken off at a gallop, hooping and hollering like some bush jockey on picnic day.

Though appalled at her unladylike antics, he'd still gunned the engine and had chased after the minx, certain in the knowledge that any car could easily outrun even the fastest racehorse in the long curving uphill driveway.

And what had she done? Jumped the darned fence and gone straight across the paddocks, scattering mares and foals as she'd leapt fence after fence like the mad daredevil she was. She'd been there waiting for him when he'd finally rounded the circular gravel driveway in front of the house, her dark eyes sparkling at him.

'You'll have to drive faster than that next time, Bill,' she'd teased. 'Or get yourself a sports car!'

It was the first time she'd called him Bill. Before that, he'd at least been Mr Sinclair.

When he'd spotted Hilary standing on the veranda of the house, glaring down at her daughter, he'd experienced some satisfaction that the brazen creature would be suitably chastised for her cheek and foolhardiness.

But what had Hilary done?

Chided the girl for losing her hat!

'Do you want to end up with skin cancer?' she'd snapped. 'Go back and find it and put the thing on, girl.' At which, the bold hussy had whirled her horse and, with another hoop and holler, set off exactly the way she'd come, jumping fence after fence.

When William had dared make some critical comment himself about the girl's recklessness, Hilary had levelled a steely gaze his way.

'Would you have said that if she'd been a boy?' she'd challenged. 'No! You'd have praised a boy's horsemanship, marvelled at his nerve, been impressed by his courage. My daughter needs those qualities in even greater quantities than any boy if she is to take over from me when I'm gone. The world of horse-breeding is a man's world, William. Courtney needs a loose rein to become the sort of woman who can survive in such a world. There's no room for sissies around here. As my heir, she will need more than a man's name. She will need a man's spirit. A man's strength. A man's ego. I aim to make sure she acquires all three.'

And you did a good job, Hilary, William thought now. The girl certainly has courage. And character, for want of a better word. But will she have enough to get out of the spot you left her in?

William gave it to Courtney straight, as requested.

Courtney listened to the very *very* bad news. Not only had her mum borrowed to buy Goldplated, as she'd feared, but to buy Four-Leaf Clover as well. And that horse had cost a small fortune! Worse, it turned out Four-Leaf Clover had not been insured, so when he'd died, the loss had been total and none of the original loan repaid.

'Your mother didn't believe in insuring anything against death,' the accountant informed Courtney, 'and I could never persuade her otherwise. As you know, she carried no life insurance herself.'

Courtney nodded. 'Yes, I know,' she said, a lump forming in her throat as the reality of her mother's death washed over her again.

Hilary's heart attack had come as such a shock to everyone, despite her being seventy last birthday. She'd always seemed so strong...

Courtney frowned. Had this escalating debt been a contributing factor in her mother's coronary? Had she been worried sick about the loan?

She'd never said a word. But then, she wouldn't have. She'd have been too proud to admit to being so foolish.

Thinking of her mother again brought a lump to Courtney's throat and a stinging to her eyes. She coughed, blinked, then gathered herself. Her mother had always hated her to cry. *Tears achieve nothing, girl. Get out and do something to fix whatever's bothering you. Don't sit there blubbering and feeling sorry for yourself!*

'Exactly how much money do I owe?' she asked brusquely.

The way Bill cleared *his* throat before answering was not a good sign. 'Er...three million dollars, give or take a thousand or two.'

Three *million*!

Courtney struggled to hide her shock. And, somehow, she managed.

'Never let the bastards know what you're thinking and feeling,' Hilary had told her more than once. 'Let your guard down, and they'll take advantage of you.'

The bastards, Courtney knew, were all men. And whilst she had not grown up to be the rabid man-hater her mother had been, she was learning to appreciate, first-hand, where her mother had been coming from when she'd lectured her daughter over the predatory nature of the male sex.

The month since the funeral had been an education, all right. She couldn't count the men who'd come out of the woodwork since she'd inherited Crosswinds, smarmily flattering her and asking if there was any way they could help, now that she was all alone in the world, *poor little thing*.

Courtney's thoughts turned wry. They wouldn't come sniffing around if they knew this poor little thing was three million dollars in debt!

Pity she couldn't tell them.

Pride, however, would keep her silent on the subject. Pride and loyalty to her mother. Hilary had spent a lifetime earning the respect of her peers in the horse-breeding world. No way would she let them laugh at her now, especially the men.

But what on earth was she going to do?

'I know it's a lot of money,' Bill said gently. 'I did try to advise your mother not to borrow any more, but she simply wouldn't listen to me.'

Courtney nodded. She understood exactly how stubborn her mother had been, and was determined not to do the same. Bill might be getting on in years but he was an intelligent man, with an old-fashioned integrity she both admired and respected. He would never try to take advantage of her, or give her bad advice. He wasn't one of the bastards. Courtney liked him enormously.

'Is the bank calling in the loan, Bill? Is that it?'

'No. They've been amazingly patient, and suspiciously generous in lending your mother more money, possibly because she had such excellent collateral against any loan. They can't lose, no matter what. Let's face it, Courtney, Crosswinds is worth a lot more than three million.'

Courtney felt the first stirrings of real alarm. 'Are you saying Crosswinds is at risk here? That one day I might have to sell up?'

'If things keep going the way they're going, and you don't try to stem the rising tide of this loan, then I'm afraid such an occurrence will be inevitable. The bank will do it for you.'

Courtney just sat there, staring at him.

How could she bear to live without Crosswinds? The

house. The horses. The land. It was all she knew and loved. It was her lifeblood. She would die without it.

Real pity for the girl swept through William. He hated having to do this so soon after her mother's death, but such things couldn't wait. A loan as large as this grew every day, especially now that interest rates were on the rise again. That loan was like the sword of Damocles, swaying over Courtney's head.

'If you want my opinion,' he said firmly, 'then you should sell some of the horses. And quickly. You have some very valuable brood mares at Crosswinds.'

A scathing look crossed the girl's face.

'Sell the brood mares? Are you mad? Do you know how long it took my mother and her family before her to breed up such stock? The brood mares are the backbone of Crosswinds. They are *in*valuable. I'd sell myself before I sold a single one of them!'

William smothered a sigh. Oh, yes. She was a chip off the old block all right. That was exactly what Hilary had said when he'd suggested the same thing a few days before her heart attack, right down to the bit about selling herself first.

He'd refrained from telling Hilary she was hardly a saleable commodity.

But her daughter was a different matter. As William's male gaze roved over the girl before him, a startling picture popped into his mind, that of a bound and naked Courtney standing proudly on some white slave trader's auction block, her magnificent black hair spread out over her bared shoulders, her beautiful brown eyes blazing defiance at the lust-filled bidders leering up at her.

What a price she would command! He could well imagine some billionaire sheikh paying a king's ransom to install Courtney Cross in his harem.

Did such things happen these days? he speculated. Possibly. But not here, in Australia.

Still, it did give William the germ of an idea…

Courtney got hold of her temper with difficulty. But, truly, Bill didn't know what he was talking about. He might know money, but he knew nothing about horses.

'How long do you think I've got?' she demanded to know. 'How long before the bank starts jumping up and down? One year? Two? Dare I hope for three?'

William suspected the bank in question might carry such a mortgage indefinitely—till it would take more than a miracle for Courtney to extricate herself from debt. In the end, they'd foreclose, and Crosswinds would be sold off, including Courtney's precious brood mares. The trouble was, in such a fire sale, nothing brought its true value. If Courtney wasn't careful, she'd not only lose Crosswinds, but there wouldn't be anything left over for her to live on. She'd be penniless.

He had to force the girl to do something *now*, or all might be lost in the future.

'It'll be the first of August this Saturday,' he said. 'I'd say you might have till the end of the year.'

'But that isn't enough time!' she protested. 'You'll have to talk to the bank, Bill, explain to them that in another couple of years I'm going to have a fantastic lot of yearlings to sell. Mum might have been foolish in some things but she was a great judge of horseflesh. Goldplated is going to be a success. I just know it. Within three years, Crosswinds will have money to burn.'

William sighed. He'd heard that one before. From Hilary. Over the years, he'd learnt that there was no such thing as a sure thing regarding racehorses, either on the track or in breeding.

'Courtney,' he said sternly, 'you must find a way to pay back that loan. And soon.'

'Well, don't go telling me to sell my horses again,' she threw at him, her face set into a mutinous expression, 'because I'm not going to. And that's final! There has to be some other way.'

'I can think of only two other solutions to your problem. Although, come to think of it, only one is viable,' he added drily.

What multi-millionaire would want to actually marry this difficult, stubborn, bossy girl? Beauty alone would not cut it, especially her kind of beauty which was of the wild and natural kind. Wealthy men wanted glamorous, well-groomed wives who stroked their egos and hosted perfect dinner parties, not independent, prickly creatures with an attitude, as well as a money problem.

'What?' Courtney's right foot hit the ground as she hunched forward on the chair, all ears. 'Tell me.'

'You'll have to find yourself a business partner, someone who'll pay cash for a share in Crosswinds.'

Pulling a face, Courtney straightened up in the chair. 'Nope. That won't work, Bill. No horseman would buy a share in Crosswinds and keep his hands off the running of the place. Mum would turn in her grave. And I wouldn't like it, either.'

'I wasn't talking about a horseman,' William explained. 'I was talking about a professional businessman. A city man. He would be a silent partner.'

'Oh, well, now that's the kind of partner I could just about tolerate. So how would I go about finding such a stooge?'

William winced at the word 'stooge'. But it probably described any potential partner of Courtney's to a tee.

'I was thinking that you could ask Lois's help. She's

a clever woman, not just at training horses but in public
relations. She's a whiz at getting money out of people
for her racing syndicates. She also has some very wealthy
clients and a wide range of contacts in the business
world. I would think Lois knows quite a few likely candidates with more money than sense.'

William saw the girl's nostrils flare indignantly. 'Are
you saying that a man would have to be stupid to go into
partnership with me?'

His smile was wry. 'Not you personally. But a wise
old accountant once told me never to invest money into
anything that had to be fed or watered.'

Courtney sighed. 'You're right. Breeding racehorses *is*
a risky investment. This businessman is going to have to
be one hell of a rich businessman.'

'Businessmen who get mixed up with racehorses in
any aspect usually are, aren't they?'

'True, Bill. True. Look, I can't say I fancy taking a
partner, even a silent one, but what must be must be.
Better than selling any of the horses. I'll give Lois a ring
as soon as I get home. I could hitch a ride down in the
horse float this Friday. I'm sending down a couple of
young horses she's agreed to syndicate out and train for
me. Darned good types, too, but obviously Crosswinds
can't afford to pay for them to be trained right now.'

'I'm afraid not,' William confirmed, relieved that
Courtney was taking it all so well. Still, he wouldn't have
expected Hilary's daughter to fall apart.

'I can't stay away too long, you know. Come this
weekend, foals will start arriving.'

'You have staff to handle that. Finding a partner is
more important, Courtney.'

'Mmm. Before I go, what about insurance? I don't
want to make the same mistake Mum did.'

'I insured everything after your mother died,' William confessed. 'I didn't want to bother you at the time for permission. I hope you don't mind.'

Courtney smiled as she rose to her feet, extending her hand across the desk. 'Not at all. Thanks, Bill. I don't know what I'd do without you.'

He flinched at the steely strength in her handshake. No wonder the horses she rode did as they were told.

'There's no trouble with our general running expenses, is there?' she asked.

'No. Cash input is matching output at the moment. Of course, the place could do with some money spent on it. It's beginning to look run down. So if you and Lois are going to sting some city fool for three million, you might as well try for four, and be done with it.'

She grinned at him. 'Bill! You shock me.'

'I doubt that very much,' he remarked drily. 'By the way, if Lois can't come up with anyone suitable, I suggest you approach a financial consultancy which specialises in handling country-based investments. But that's a last resort. Middlemen always want their cut. A personal contact deal would be much better all round.'

'I agree. If I have to have a partner, then I'd like to have some control over who it is. Now, I'd better get moving. Friday will be here before I know it.'

'Good luck, Courtney.'

'See you, Bill.'

She spun on the heels of her elastic-sided boots and had taken three strides towards the door when she stopped and threw a puzzled glance back over her shoulder at him. 'What was the other one?' she asked.

'What other one?'

'The other solution to my money problems.'

'Oh, that. It was a stupid idea. Not worth mentioning.'

She turned right round again with that stubborn set to her face he knew so well. 'I'd still like to know.'

William let out a resigned sigh. 'I was thinking of what impoverished aristocratic women used to do in the old days when their castles were crumbling around them.'

'What's that?'

'They married for money.'

Courtney crowed with laughter. 'You're right, Bill. That is the stupidest idea I've ever heard of. I think the world has moved on since the days when young ladies went round sacrificing themselves in marriage to aging pot-bellied counts, simply to save the family jewels.'

Actually, William wasn't too sure of that.

'If and when I marry,' Courtney announced as she planted the dusty Akubra hat firmly on her head, 'it won't be for money.'

'Ah-h-h.' William smiled his approval. 'For love, eh, girl?'

'Don't be ridiculous, Bill. Love won't have anything to do with it. It'll be strictly for the sex.' And, smiling a truly wicked smile, she whirled and strode from the room.

CHAPTER TWO

'EVERYONE'S very dressed up,' Courtney said, glancing around at the crowd of racegoers.

All the men were in suits and ties, and most of the women were wearing hats. Lois herself was in a rather flamboyant floral suit and matching hat which might have looked over-the-top on anyone less slender and vivacious. But she carried the outfit off with great panache, looking a lot younger than the forty she admitted to.

'I did warn you, darling,' Lois replied. 'Randwick is a far cry from a country racetrack.'

'You can say that again. Thanks heaps for lending me these clothes, Lois. Sorry I was stubborn about it.'

Lois rolled her eyes. She'd had the devil of a time persuading the girl out of the jeans and checked shirt she'd been wearing this morning, and into the stylish black pants and matching cropped jacket she now had on. This minor miracle had only been achieved by her firmly telling Courtney that the members' section at Randwick had a dress code that definitely didn't allow jeans.

As for that revolting checked shirt... Lois shuddered at the memory.

Lois had learnt many years ago that, in the city, appearance was everything. Just because you were a horse trainer it didn't mean you had to look like one. Lois spent an absolute fortune on her vibrant but stylish clothes, and the expenditure was worth every penny. The press photographers snapped her all the time, and the media were always seeking her opinion on the chances of her horses, possibly because she looked better on TV than most of the male trainers. She talked better, too. And smiled a lot. Lois believed that acting bright and always sounding positive brought her more coverage and more clients than the actual success of her horses.

'You look fantastic in black,' she complimented Courtney. 'Much better than I ever did.' Actually, black hadn't been her colour since she'd had her hair blonded last year. It looked great on Hilary's daughter, however, with her olive skin, black hair and almost black eyes. If the girl had agreed to some red lipstick and to leaving that gorgeous hair of hers down, she'd have been simply stunning. But, when Lois had suggested both this morning, Courtney had bluntly stated that she looked like a clown in make-up and simply couldn't stand her hair around her face.

Lois had argued her case but the girl was adamant. Clearly, she was as opinionated and strong-willed as her mother. Lois had put her foot down, however, when Courtney had gone to scoop her gorgeous black curls back up into that awful rubber band, and had insisted that if her hair had to be off her face, it should be anchored more attractively at the nape of her neck with a gold clip.

Courtney had finally shrugged and given in, as though it didn't really matter either way. Lois could only conclude that Hilary's daughter had no idea of the uniquely exotic beauty she possessed, and which would have more than one wealthy man slavering at her feet if only she knew what to do with it.

Still, what could one expect? Teaching her daughter to make the most of her striking looks would not have been high on Hilary's agenda. Such a stupid, warped old woman. Why hate men when they ran the world?

Tonight, over dinner, she would try to explain to Courtney that when a woman did business in a man's world, she did it as much with her body as her brain. If Courtney wanted to save Crosswinds, then she would hopefully listen to reason.

If not, then it would be up to herself to rescue the darned place single-handed, Lois decided pragmatically. No way was she going to sit back and let that wonderful old property pass into other hands. Crosswinds had the best staying brood mares in Australia. All they needed was the right sire, and a whole crop of champion colts and fillies would be in the making. And she would be right there, willing and eager to train every single one of the little darlings!

Courtney wasn't enjoying her trip to the races as much as she'd thought she would. Her mind was still on Crosswinds and her money problems.

'Do you think we might meet someone here today, Lois?' she asked tautly.

'Someone to bail Crosswinds out, you mean?'

'Yes.'

'Possibly. Though this isn't all that major a race meeting. Not too many of the seriously rich here today. Look, darling, take my advice and don't go worrying about Crosswinds this afternoon. Just relax and enjoy yourself. Tonight, after dinner, I'll sit down and make a list of likely candidates, then tomorrow I'll ring around and issue some invitations.'

'What kind of invitations?'

'Dinner. Drinks. Whatever suits each man in question.'

'You don't know any suitably rich women?' Rich women liked racehorses too, Courtney had been thinking. And there would be less chance of a woman partner wanting to interfere with the management of Crosswinds. She just didn't trust a man not to try to poke his bib in.

Lois looked just a tad exasperated. 'Lord, darling, no woman is going to want to be *your* partner. You're far too good-looking. No, no, no, some filthy rich old bloke is our best bet. Trust me. By the end of the week, we'll come up with just the right person. I have every confid— Oh, good God, it's Jack Falconer. And he said he definitely wasn't going to be here today!'

Courtney followed the direction of Lois's disgruntled gaze and encountered a man standing at the railing of the saddling enclosure, alternately studying the race book in his hands, then the horses being led around the parade ring. A pair of expensive-looking binoculars were hooked around his neck. He was tall, with a strongly masculine profile and close-cropped dark hair.

Courtney's eyebrows lifted. She'd always fancied macho-looking men, and this one was certainly that, despite his sleek, city-smooth clothes. He was somewhere in his early thirties, she guessed. Though she couldn't be certain from this distance. He could have been older.

His being older wouldn't have made him any less attractive to Courtney. She liked older men.

'Who's Jack Falconer?' she asked, intrigued by Lois's reaction to seeing him.

'What? Oh...one of my owners.'

'Rich?'

'Used to be. Not so rich any more.'

'What happened?'

'He chose the *wrong* business partner. The mongrel embezzled a good chunk of their clients' money and did a flit to Paraguay or Bolivia, or wherever. Jack nobly made restitution himself, though legally he didn't have to, and it almost sent him to the wall. He lost just about everything, including his live-in lady. The rotten cow dumped him and married a politician old enough to be her father. Rolling in dough, of course. Jack pretended he wasn't shattered but he clearly was. He was besotted with his darling Katrina. He only bought a share in a racehorse in the first place because she loved coming to the races and mingling with the rich and famous.'

'She sounds awful. Whatever did he see in her?'

Lois laughed. 'When you see her, you'll know the answer to that. And you'll see her today. Her new hubby is presenting the trophy in the main race of the day. That's why I was so taken aback to see Jack here. Because his... Oh, darn, he's spotted me. I'll fill you in later.'

Lois plastered a high-voltage beam on her face and stepped off the veranda of the members' stand into the warm winter sunshine. Courtney followed, more intrigued than ever by the man walking towards Lois. Full frontal and up closer, he was even more attractive, with the sort of deep-set blue eyes that Courtney adored.

No grey in his dark brown hair that she could see, so her guess of early thirties remained. As did her initial impression that he was really built. With his suit jacket flapping open and his tie blown back over his right shoulder, there was no hiding the way his broad chest was stretching the material of his pale blue shirt.

Yet there was no question of fat, or flab. That telling area around his waistline against which his binoculars kept bouncing as he walked showed no hint of a soft underbelly, or of being held in. His stomach looked flat and rock-hard, just the way Courtney liked them.

He was even taller than she'd first thought on seeing him standing alone in the distance. Six four at least. A big man all round.

Courtney adored big men.

The three of them met on the grass, with Courtney hanging back slightly. All the better to observe him from…

'Jack, darling…' Lois presented her cheek to him for a kiss. 'How lovely to see you.'

'Hello, Lois.' He smiled with a slightly crooked smile as he bent to give her a peck. 'You're looking lovely today. There again, you always look lovely.'

'You're such a flatterer,' she said coyly, and Courtney tried not to laugh. But the woman was a riot. As rough as guts around the stables, but here, at the races, butter wouldn't melt in her mouth.

'Now, what are you doing here, Jack?' Lois went on sweetly. 'When I contacted you this week, you said you definitely wouldn't be. What changed your mind? The glorious weather?'

He seemed drily amused by her none too subtle probing. 'No, after we talked I remembered you always said that the first time you put Big Brutus over a bit of distance, he'd win.'

'He will too,' Lois replied. 'I'm very confident.'

Recognition of the horse's name dragged Courtney's attention away from ogling Jack Falconer. Big Brutus was one of Four-Leaf Clover's first crop and the ugliest colt her mother had ever bred. Hence his name. He'd been one of the yearlings she'd refused to sell for peanuts, subsequently leasing him to Lois. He'd been a total dud at two years old, not much better at three, and had turned four this very day, still with only a few minor placings.

But he was bred to stay all day.

Courtney scrambled through her race book to find the

race Big Brutus was entered in. There it was. A handicap over twenty-four-hundred metres, with prize money of...

'Wow!' she exclaimed. 'First place pays a hundred thousand smackeroos. My cut would be what, Lois?'

Those piercing blue eyes swung her way. 'I beg your pardon? God, don't tell me you're Big Brutus's jockey. Tell me she's not the jockey, Lois.'

'She's not the jockey,' Lois said with a wry smile on her face. 'But if she was, you'd have one of the best riders in the country on your horse.'

'That may be, but I've never had much luck betting on female jockeys.'

Courtney bristled in defence of her sex. And irritation at herself for once again being attracted to a male chauvinist. Would she never find a man who looked as she liked them to look, yet believed God created man and woman equal?

'When a race is lost,' she said frostily, 'it's mostly the horse's fault. Or the trainer's. Or the owner's. Not the jockey, be she female or otherwise.'

'I don't see how it can be the owner's fault,' he argued back.

'Some owners insist on seeing their horses run in races far above their talents. And other owners insist their horses not run up to their ability at all!'

'Courtney,' Lois whispered under her breath.

'No, no, let her finish,' Jack insisted. 'Do go on, Ms...er...?'

'Cross,' she announced.

'Yes, I can see that,' he said, smiling.

Courtney would have liked to wipe that smirk off his face with more than her tongue. But she hadn't physically brawled with a member of the opposite sex since she was thirteen, and didn't think the lawns at Royal Randwick Racecourse was the place to begin again.

'Aside from the horse having a lousy trainer or a crooked owner,' she continued tartly, 'the main reason female jockeys don't ride all that many winners is that they are rarely offered the best rides in races, and when they are their male counterparts make sure none of the breaks go their way. It's a sad fact of life that the male sex do not appreciate women taking them on in fields they've always considered their own private turf.'

'Possibly. But you must concede that pound for pound male jockeys are stronger. Take you, for instance. If you were a jockey, quite a few pounds of your riding weight would be wasted on your very nice but less than useful breasts. Strength-wise, that is,' he added ruefully.

'Actually, no, that's not the case,' she countered without batting an eye. It wasn't the first time Courtney had heard that old argument. It had whiskers on it. 'If I were riding professionally, I'd have to strip off at least twenty pounds and my boobs would shrink from their present cup C to a flat-chested double A. Add five hundred push-ups a day, and I'd be every bit as strong as any male jockey. Being female is not the point here. It's a matter of talent and opportunity. A woman jockey can have all the talent in the world, but rarely gets the opportunities.'

He smiled. 'I give up. You win.'

'Thank you,' she said crisply, but didn't smile back. She was still smarting inside for finding him so attractive, and wasn't about to be won over by one smarmy little smile.

Getting the message that he was on the outer, he turned to Lois. 'So explain the mystery to me, Lois? Why is Ms Cross, here, entitled to a share of Big Brutus's prize money?'

'Courtney's mother bred Big Brutus. I leased him as a yearling, then syndicated him out to you and your partner.'

'Oh, I see. Sorry,' he directed at Courtney with another winning smile. 'And sorry about the jockey bit. I was only stirring. I don't know about your riding talents, but your debating skills are excellent. You wouldn't be a budding lady-lawyer by any chance?'

His charm was undeniable, and Courtney struggled to stay angry with him.

'Courtney is a horse breeder, too,' Lois answered for her. 'The Crosses have been breeding thoroughbreds for generations.'

'You don't look like a horse breeder,' he said, and those sexy blue eyes raked over her from top to toe.

Courtney's heart lurched upwards, then did a swallow dive down into her stomach.

Wow, she thought a bit dazedly. This guy is dynamite.

'Since Lois isn't going to introduce me properly,' he said, 'then I will. Jack Falconer...' And he held out his hand.

It was a big hand, naturally. He was a big man.

Reaching out, she slid her own relatively small hand against his huge palm, curling her thumb around half of his and squeezing firmly.

'Courtney Cross,' she replied, steadfastly ignoring her madly galloping heart.

'Delighted.' And he squeezed even more firmly back.

She felt it all the way down to her toes.

Courtney simply could not understand how any woman with an active libido could prefer some aging politician to this gorgeous hunk of male flesh.

The only possible answer was money.

Okay, so he'd fallen on hard times. But not through any fault of his own, according to Lois.

Courtney wondered how he could afford Big Brutus's training fees. Lois didn't come cheap.

'And what is it you do for a crust, Jack?' she asked, not subscribing to the theory that you never asked personal questions on first acquaintance. How else were you going to find out what you wanted to know?

'I used to be a financial consultant,' he said happily enough. 'Or an investment broker, if you prefer that label. At the moment, I'm a gentleman of leisure.'

'You mean you're unemployed.'

'Courtney!' Lois broke in. 'For heaven's sake.'

'It's perfectly all right, Lois,' Jack said. 'I don't mind. If by unemployed you mean I don't work for wages, then you're absolutely right. I am unemployed in that sense. But I'm not broke. And I'm not on the dole. Currently, I am a man of independent means.'

Which meant he was looking for work and living on his savings.

'Would you two excuse me for a few minutes?' Lois interrupted. 'I've just spotted the owners of my horse in the second race. Jack, darling, look after Courtney for me, will you? Take her inside, up into the bar overlooking the track. Get her a drink. I'll find you when I'm finished down here.'

Courtney was not displeased at being left alone with the dishy Jack. But, as Lois walked off, he looked momentarily disconcerted.

'You don't mind, do you?' she said straight away.

His eyes cleared of the cloud that had momentarily muddied them to a bleak grey. 'Why should I mind?'

'Maybe you want to go place a bet on the first race,'

she said. 'Or maybe you have other friends here that you feel you should be getting back to.'

'No. Not at all.'

'What about the other part-owner of Big Brutus?'

'He's in Bolivia. I now own all of Big Brutus.'

'Oh! I didn't realise Lois meant that partner. I wasn't listening properly.' She'd been too busy ogling Jack. 'Owning a racehorse all by yourself is very expensive, you know. Can you afford it?'

'I will be able to, after today. Lois is confident Big Brutus is going to win.'

'Lois is always confident her horses are going to win, especially when there's a cup or a prize at stake.'

Jack smiled a lazy smile. 'She is, isn't she?'

'Still, often enough she's right. She does love those trophies. My mother thought her quite wonderful.'

'*Thought?*'

Courtney swallowed. 'My mum passed away recently.' It still hurt, but the urge to cry whenever she thought about, or talked of her mother was gradually lessening. In a dozen years or so, she might actually get over losing her mentor, and champion.

'I'm sorry,' Jack said gently. 'Had she been ill? She couldn't have been very old. Unless you're the youngest in the family.'

'Actually, she was quite old. Seventy. I was her only child, born when she was forty-five.'

'Goodness. And your father?'

'My father is not a part of my life,' she said with an indifferent shrug. 'I never knew him, you see, and Mum rarely spoke of him, except in general and not very flattering terms. But gossip put him a good deal younger than her. A gypsy seducer, I gleaned from my classmates at school. And others over the years.'

'Ah. Good old gossip. It never lets the truth get in the way of a good story. He was possibly a very nice man.'

Somehow, Courtney doubted that. A very nice man would not have made her mother so bitter. But his absence had never hurt *her*. She'd rather relished the freedom of not having some male hand controlling her upbringing. People said her mother had let her run wild. That wasn't entirely true. The wildness, Courtney believed, she'd been born with.

'But let's not dwell on sadness,' Jack said, hooking his right arm through her left. 'Let's go and have that drink Lois suggested.'

'Yes, let's,' Courtney agreed, delighted to have the company of this very stimulating man.

The table he steered her to in the upstairs bar had a perfect view of the track. She could see the horses trotting out for the first race. But she didn't watch them for long. Her eyes were all on Jack as he went over to get the drinks himself rather than wait to be served at the table.

'Will you be going back into the investment business again?' was her first question when he returned with two glasses of champagne.

'Possibly.'

'I might be in need of an investment broker soon,' she said.

'Why would that be?' Jack asked, frowning.

'To find me a silent partner. For my stud farm. Not that I like the idea. Unfortunately, it's a necessity.'

'You have a money problem?'

Courtney rolled her eyes. 'Do I have a money problem?'

'Tell me about it.'

Courtney could see no reason why she shouldn't tell him. If Lois didn't come through with someone, she just might give him a call. Besides, she fancied him rotten and there was interest in his eyes.

So she told him. Everything. All her mother's mistakes and misfortunes over the last few years. Even the amount of money she now owed and needed to find.

'Lois thinks she'll find some suitably mega-rich businessman from amongst her wealthy racing contacts,' she finished up. 'And she probably will, knowing Lois. But I'm not so sure it's a good idea to take on a partner who's mad about racing and who might develop some private fantasies about becoming a hands-on breeder himself. I'd prefer someone who just looks on this as a financial deal.'

'Fair enough. Have you told Lois that?'

'I've only just starting thinking that way. It's difficult to think straight when you're desperate.'

'Never be desperate, Courtney. Being desperate is the way to disaster. People know when you're desperate and take advantage of you. Always be cool. Never show fear. I'm sure you'd be very good at that.'

Courtney was impressed. It was the sort of advice her mother would have given her.

'You're right,' she said. 'There's no need to panic. The bank hasn't actually foreclosed as yet. So what do you suggest I do?' she asked.

'Take your time in finding just the right person. If the bank hasn't sent out any warning or threatening letters, then desperation hour has not yet arrived. Don't rush into anything. Scout around. I could give you the names of some very good investment brokerages here in Sydney. Ring them up and go see them.'

'How long will that take?'

'How long have you got?'

'I really have to get back to Crosswinds as quickly as I can. It's foaling time and I'm short-staffed. My accountant says this is more important, but he just doesn't understand.'

'It would take at least a week to line up appointments and do the rounds,' Jack said.

'Would you help me? I mean…a personal introduction would be much better than my just ringing up these people out of the blue.'

He seemed a little taken aback by her request.

'You did say you were a gentleman of leisure,' Courtney pointed out with a decidedly flirtatious smile.

He smiled back, if a little ruefully. 'You have a hide, Ms Cross. Has anyone ever told you that?'

'Several people, actually.'

'I'm not surprised. But, okay, I guess I could do worse things with my time than squire a beautiful young woman around town. Have you been down to Sydney before? Or is this your first visit?'

'Lord, no, I've been lots of times over the years. And frankly I'm always happy to get home to Crosswinds.'

'You don't like the city?'

'Can't say that I do. What you see is not always what you get.'

'So young to be a cynic.'

'Is there a right age to see through hypocrisy?'

'I guess not…' He looked thoughtfully down into his champagne for a few moments before glancing back up. He opened his mouth to say something, but closed it again with no words coming out. His blue eyes grew arctic-cold, then colder still, his gaze fixed on something beyond Courtney's shoulder.

Female intuition warned her that only one person could cause this reaction. The treacherous Katrina. The woman who'd ditched him and married another man; the woman Lois said he was still besotted with.

But that didn't look like love glittering in Jack's chilling blue eyes. It was more like hate. Hate, and the need for vengeance.

CHAPTER THREE

WHAT kind of woman, Courtney puzzled as she sat there, could inspire such strong emotions in a man like Jack Falconer?

If Courtney had been alone, she'd have simply spun round in her chair and taken a good, long, hard look. But this situation called for a bit more subtlety, despite the fact that subtlety was not her strong suit.

She improvised. 'I need to go to the loo. I won't be long.' Standing up, she turned and pretended to search the room for the ladies' whilst zeroing in on the direction of Jack's piercing gaze.

And there she was, standing by the bar, clinging to the arm of a white-haired gentleman whose suit jacket was struggling to remain done up over his portly stomach.

Courtney had no doubts it was Katrina.

Lois had said she would understand Jack's infatuation once Courtney saw her. And she did.

Katrina would have given any supermodel in the world a run for her money. She had everything they had, and possibly more. The height. The figure. The face. The hair. Definitely the clothes.

She was wearing a superbly cut calf-length cream woollen dress which hugged her stream-lined body, revealing every flowing but delectable curve. Her hair, which was a similar cream colour, was worn up in a rather severe French pleat which served to emphasise the perfection of her classically beautiful face. Gold and diamond earrings winked in her lobes. Her neck was bare, perhaps because she didn't want to distract any man's eyes from its elegant length, and the impressive cleavage the dress's deep V-neckline put on display.

Courtney couldn't see the colour of her eyes from that distance but she could certainly see the colour of her mouth. A rich blood-red.

Jack's blood, she thought angrily.

Seeing the man Katrina had chosen over Jack, however, confirmed Courtney's guess that this was all a matter of money. Katrina had obviously wanted to marry money, and Jack no longer had enough. What a cold-hearted money-grubbing bitch!

'The ladies' room is over there,' Jack said, misinterpreting her lengthy hesitation.

Courtney whirled back to face him. He'd sounded totally composed, but his eyes betrayed emotions best not explored. 'Where?'

He pointed to a far corner.

Courtney quickly assessed that there were two routes she could use to make her way there. One went straight between the tables, the other skirted the bar. Courtney went between the tables on her way there, and skirted the bar on her way back. Superbitch was still there, sipping a cocktail and hanging on hubby's every word.

'Hi, Katrina,' Courtney said breezily as she passed, but without stopping. Long enough, however, to see the cow's green eyes—they would be green, wouldn't they?—lift in surprise, then trail after her.

Courtney threw Jack a blinder of a smile as she walked towards him, and he automatically smiled back, as she had known he would. 'You were quick,' he said once she'd sat down again.

'Didn't have to touch up my make-up,' she said truthfully. 'Or my hair.'

He gave her face and hair a long, thoughtful look. 'You don't need to. You look great.'

'Thanks. You look great too.'

His laughter was real, and his eyes warm with genuine amusement. 'You are a very unique girl, do you know that?'

'Yep.'

He laughed again. 'Didn't your mother ever teach you modesty?'

'Lord, no. She taught me to say what I thought and do what I pleased.'

Jack's straight dark brows shot upwards. 'A very unusual mother, from the sounds of things.'

'She was.'

'You must tell me more about her. And about yourself. But first, I think another drink is—'

When he broke off, his eyes freezing once more, Courtney knew the reason why. She'd bargained on Katrina watching where she went, then not being able to resist coming over. It was one thing to dump a man. Quite another to find him seemingly happy in the company of another woman. And a much younger woman, at that.

If there was one thing guaranteed to get up the nose of a thirty-something female, it was seeing *her* ex with a younger woman.

And Courtney wanted to get up Katrina's oh, so perfect nose to the nth degree.

'Jack,' came a softly purring voice which could belong to none other but the scheming cow herself. 'I didn't expect to see you here today.'

She drifted into Courtney's view. Hubby, however, was nowhere in sight.

Jack smiled a smile that sent shivers running down

Courtney's spine. Here was a man who would not forgive
easily. Or forget. It occurred to her that Jack's embez-
zling partner would be wise to stay exiled for ever in his
South American hide-away.

'Why ever not, Katrina?' Jack drawled, leaning his
broad shoulders back against his chair. 'Big Brutus is
going to win today and I'm going to be there to accept
the trophy. Along with Courtney, here.'

Glittering green eyes swung her way. 'I'm sorry,'
Katrina said with lemony sweetness. 'You said hello to
me, but I can't seem to place you.'

'Oh, you don't actually know me,' Courtney trilled
back. 'But I feel like I know you. Jack has told me *so*
much about you.'

'Really,' Katrina said coldly.

'We didn't want to have any secrets between us, did
we, Jack?' Courtney smiled over at Jack, who thankfully
wasn't looking too poleaxed by her bold charade.

'How nice,' his ex managed to grate out between her
dazzlingly white but grindingly clenched teeth. 'So how
long have you two been going out together?'

'Gosh, I'm not sure,' Courtney jumped in again. 'I
haven't been counting. How long has it been, darling?'
By now, she hoped and prayed Jack would back up her
story.

'Lord knows, sweetheart,' he returned, his eyes
amused on her. 'I haven't been counting, either. All I
know is it's been one remarkable experience.'

Courtney could practically *feel* the woman's hostility.
If she gripped her purse any tighter, her scarlet fingernails
would sink holes in the leather.

'She's a little young for you, don't you think, Jack?'
Katrina sniped.

Jack's expression was superbly indifferent to the

woman's barb. What a man, Courtney thought. City-smooth and city-smart. But with such adorably macho looks. A most unusual combination.

'I would have thought she's just the right age,' he replied coolly. 'Can't say the same for old George, however. He's only got a few good years left in him, I would imagine. Look, I'd love to chat, Katrina, but the horses are in the barrier. We're sure to run into each other later, after Big Brutus wins his race, since George is going to present the trophy.'

With that, Jack picked up his binoculars from the table and focused them on the race that had just jumped. Katrina glared pure hate at Courtney, then stalked off.

'She's gone,' Courtney whispered, smiling satisfaction to herself.

'I'm not sure if I should be angry with you, or grateful,' Jack muttered drily, but without shifting his eyes away from the binoculars.

'Grateful would be the more sensible option.'

'I presume Lois told you about Katrina.'

'Only the bare facts. I asked her if you were rich and she told me of your own recent money troubles, which led on to her mentioning Katrina's defection to George.'

'Ah... I see... Yes... That explains everything.'

He fell silent then, seemingly intent on the race. It was only a sprint and the runners were already approaching the turn into the straight, with three of them vying for the lead and another pair hot on their heels. It looked like being an exciting finish.

Yet, for the first time during the running of a horse race, Courtney found her mind wandering away from the action.

A couple of things had begun puzzling her. She could understand why Jack hadn't quite got over Katrina yet.

After all, *he* was the one who'd been dumped. And the woman was simply stunning to look at. Courtney suspected she was hot stuff in bed as well.

But Katrina's jealousy on seeing Jack with another female seemed over the top. What on earth had she expected? That a man like him would never turn his eye elsewhere? Had she imagined for a moment that she was irreplaceable in Jack's life, that her betrayal would turn him into an embittered celibate?

The idea was laughable. The woman had to have a screw loose.

Unfortunately, it *did* seem as if Jack hadn't turned his eye elsewhere as yet. He'd come here today alone, hadn't he? She was just a pretend girlfriend.

'You're far better off without her, you know,' she announced with pragmatic logic just as the horses flashed past the post. 'If she didn't love you poor, then she didn't love you at all, did she?'

Jack lowered his binoculars and gave her a long, hard look. 'I know you meant well in doing what you just did, Courtney. And in a way I'm grateful to you. But you really don't know what you're talking about where Katrina and I are concerned. Neither does Lois. She…oh, oh, talk of the devil. Lois is about to descend upon us. Now, for pity's sake, don't relay to her anything that just happened. And you can drop the besotted girlfriend bit. Katrina and co have left the bar.'

Courtney pulled a face. 'Pity. I was rather enjoying myself. What about when Big Brutus wins? Shouldn't I revive the role, at least for the presentation?'

'Let's wait till the horse actually wins, shall we?' Jack stated drily. 'Hi, there, Lois. Time for a glass of champers?'

CHAPTER FOUR

'SO WHAT *do* you think, Courtney?' Jack asked ten minutes before the main race. 'Will Big Brutus win, or not?'

They were standing by the parade ring, watching the grooms leading their charges around in circles. Lois was standing in the grassed centre, giving her hoop last-minute instructions and suddenly looking very much the professional horsetrainer she was.

'Come on,' Jack persisted. 'You're the horse expert here. Give me your expert advice.'

Courtney had to admit she was impressed by Big Brutus's appearance this time in. He was beginning to look like the classy thoroughbred his breeding indicated, most of his earlier ugly angles filled in with hard muscle.

And there was that superior look in his eye which often denoted a good racehorse. Her mother had always had faith in Big Brutus and her mother had been no mean judge of horseflesh.

'He certainly looks the goods today,' she said. 'Worth a bet at the odds.' He was twelve to one.

'Mmm.' Jack reached for his wallet. 'Each way?'

'Betting each way is for little old ladies,' she scorned. 'Better to put your money straight out on two horses than wimp out on one.'

'Heaven help any man who looked a wimp in front of you!' he returned, smiling wryly. 'Straight out it will be, then. Stay where you are. I'll be back shortly.'

Courtney watched him counting out a lot of notes as

he hurried off. She hoped he wasn't going to put too much money on Big Brutus's nose. He probably couldn't afford it. Besides, her record of tipping winners wasn't all that great. Too biased, most of the time.

Strangely, she wasn't much of a gambler herself. Her thrill whenever a Crosswinds-bred horse raced was just as great with or without a bet on it. She didn't need any extra adrenaline charge. Her excitement level was already at its zenith, just watching one of their horses run around. To see it win was the ultimate joy.

Her heart contracted at this last thought. If only her mum could have been here today. She loved it when one of her horses won.

Though in this instance it was a case of *if*, not *when*.

'If you're watching from up there, Mum,' she murmured under her breath with an upward glance into the clear blue sky, 'then ask the Lord for a little help. No, a *lot* of help. This is Big Brutus here. As you know, the best he's finished so far is second. In a maiden!'

The reality of Big Brutus's past form hit home and Courtney sighed. Lois really shouldn't build people's hopes up.

By the time Jack returned to lead her up into the stand to watch the race, Big Brutus' price had tumbled to an alarming six to one.

'My God, how much money did you put on?' she questioned as they squeezed into a spot in the stands not too far from the winning post.

'Nothing I can't afford,' he returned calmly.

'Yeah, right. And if Big Brutus doesn't win? I'll bet come Monday you'll be heading for the dole queue.'

'But you said he *would* win.'

'I said no such thing!' she protested. 'I said he looked well. If you want to lose the rest of your savings on a stupid horse race, then that's your problem. I didn't twist your arm.'

'True,' he said with a smile.

He wouldn't be looking so cool when Big Brutus ran down the track, Courtney thought angrily. Men! Egotistical fools, the lot of them!

Despite her dismissal of any personal responsibility for Jack's bet, Courtney's stomach began churning and chundering like an old washing machine stuck on the spin cycle.

'They're off!' she shouted simultaneously with the course commentator, every muscle in her body tightening.

It wasn't a big field. Only ten starters. But when Big Brutus settled down at the tail soon after the start, Courtney had to stifle a groan of dismay. As much as she kept telling herself this was Randwick, where horses could come from behind once they topped the rise into the straight, Big Brutus's record in races up till now didn't help. He was a good stayer, all right. He usually *stayed* at the back of the field.

By the time they reached the back straight, with half the race already over, Big Brutus was still running last. Admittedly, the front runners were setting a brisk pace, which meant they might tire, and Big Brutus *did* look as if he was just jogging.

'Get a move on, you ugly old brute!' she burst out at long last.

'You talking about the horse or the jockey?' Jack quipped drily out of the side of his mouth.

She threw him a vicious glance, warning him that any smart alec chit-chat was not a good idea at this stage of proceedings. But he wasn't looking at her. His eyes were glued to his binoculars.

'Move him up closer,' Courtney urged loudly from the stand, cupping her hands around her mouth as though by some miracle this action would funnel the advice half a mile away.

'Now, that's definitely advice for the jockey,' Jack muttered, bringing an exasperated sigh from Courtney.

'It's *your* money going down the gurgler,' she pointed out tartly, whereupon Jack dropped his binoculars and started shouting advice as well.

They both fell deathly silent, however, when the field swung into the straight and a still trailing Big Brutus was pulled out into the centre of the track to make his run. His long legs lengthened stride and he began to gobble up his opposition. With a furlong to go, he swept past the tiring front runners.

'The ugly old brute is going to win,' Jack said with awe in his voice. 'Lois was right!'

The reality of his words snapped Courtney out of her own frozen state of shock, and she started jumping up and down. 'Go, boy, go!' she chanted like a demented rock groupie. 'Go! Go! Go!'

Big Brutus went all right, leading the field by ten lengths, stretching out his neck at the winning post as all really good racehorses do. An ecstatic Courtney threw her arms around Jack. 'He won!' she cried. 'He won!'

'He sure did,' Jack said, grinning and making no attempt to disengage her.

'You must have won a good bit,' she said, so pleased for him.

'More than a good bit. The *bookie* is going to be the one heading for the dole queue after he pays me out, I can assure you.'

'Fantastic! Lois, did you hear that? Jack won a stack on Big Brutus.'

Lois didn't hear a thing. She was too busy hugging everyone within hugging distance. It suddenly crossed Courtney's mind that Katrina was probably watching all this hoo-ha from somewhere in the crowded stand. With that thought in mind, she launched herself up on tiptoe and kissed Jack full on the mouth.

For a second or two, she thought he was going to spoil everything and push her way.

But he didn't do any such thing. He did just the opposite. He yanked her hard against him and kissed her back, kissed her with an incredibly explosive passion, kissed her till everything in her head was scattered to the four winds and there was nothing but his lips grinding against hers, his tongue deep in her mouth, and his hands burning hot through her clothes.

And then...*then* he pushed her away.

She gasped and stared up at him with startled eyes. He laughed softly, gathering her close again. She didn't resist. She *couldn't* resist.

Amazing...

'Be careful what you start wanting, Courtney Cross,' he whispered into her ear. 'Or you just might get it.'

Lois's tapping Jack on the shoulder had him drawing back once more.

'Hate to interrupt, folks,' she said, giving a flushed Courtney a raised-eye glance. 'But it's time to go lead Big Brutus in. Would you like to do the honours, Courtney?'

Courtney snapped out of her highly uncharacteristic fluster to congratulate Lois on her brilliant training of Big Brutus, grateful for the opportunity to turn her mind from Jack's kiss. She'd been dangerously turned on there for a while. And he'd known it.

Courtney never liked a man to think he had her at a

disadvantage. She liked to call the shots in every aspect of her life. And that included her sex life.

'You do realise you're leading in a Melbourne Cup contender,' Lois remarked happily as the three of them made their way downstairs.

The Melbourne Cup! Courtney had to admire Lois's optimism. Admittedly, after today, she respected the woman's judgement a good deal more. But Australia's premier staying race over two miles was a big step up from today's mediocre-class handicap.

'You've actually entered him?' Courtney asked, knowing that was not a cheap exercise in itself.

'Your mother did.'

'My God, wasn't that just like her?'

'Your mother knew what she was doing, Courtney. The horse has got a good chance. It's a handicap race, remember? Big Brutus will get in with a very light weight. Of course, he'll have to win one of the qualifying lead-up races to ensure him of a start. But he'll do that easily, after today.'

'Lord, don't say things like that in front of Jack!' Courtney exclaimed. 'Or he'll make Big Brutus favourite next time! He might even be tempted to take some of those ridiculous odds they give Melbourne Cup entries months in advance.'

It was three months till the big race itself took place, on the first Tuesday in November. A veritable lifetime in horse racing. A million things could happen to stop them even taking their place at the start!

And then there was the race itself. Twenty top stayers from all over the world vying for the biggest prize money on the Australian racing calendar, every owner trying, every jockey riding more recklessly and ruthlessly than usual.

'Tell Jack not to waste his winnings, Lois,' Courtney advised firmly. 'Tell him to wait and see how things pan out.'

'As long as Jack's paying Big Brutus's training fees,' Lois said, 'I'll be telling him the truth as I see it. Big Brutus has a good chance in the Cup, Jack. Make no mistake about that. And I'll get him to the post. Make no mistake about that, either. Your money could do worse than to ride round on such a noble animal's back.'

Courtney rolled her eyes at Jack, who tactfully smothered his laughter.

They'd barely made it downstairs and out onto the grass when a tall, balding chap with a microphone grabbed Lois for an on-the-spot television interview.

Courtney hurried over to lead Big Brutus back into the number one gate, patting his sweaty neck and telling him what a good horse he was before remembering to congratulate the jockey on his brilliantly patient ride.

'Just followed instructions,' the jockey said. 'Frankly, you could have knocked me over with a feather when he took off like he did. Never done that before. Still, now that he's hit his straps, I think the big boy will go on to better things. I'd be very happy to have the ride on him again, no matter what race he starts in.'

'What was the jockey saying to you?' Jack asked on her eventually returning to his side.

'He wants to ride Big Brutus, no matter what race he's entered in.'

'And what do *you* think?'

'I think you kiss very well.' Couldn't leave him thinking he'd really rattled her.

He shook his head, laughing. 'You're incorrigible, do you know that?'

'Agnes tells me as much, practically every day.'

'Who's Agnes?'

'She's the housekeeper at Crosswinds. She's also the woman who delivered me. Mum hired her when she was pregnant because of Agnes's midwifery skills. She didn't want any man attending to her, you see. Agnes helped raise me, too. But she gave up when I was around seven. They say that's the age of reason. Agnes claims seven was the age of my becoming *un*reasonable.'

'Perceptive woman, this Agnes.'

'Really!'

'Well, you do suffer from a serious lack of discipline and self-control. One day someone is going to have to take you in hand.'

'Mmm. Sounds kinky. Would you like to volunteer?'

'I thought I already warned you about being provocative.'

'Hey, it was your tongue halfway down my throat,' she tossed at him, 'not the other way around.'

'And weren't you loving it?'

'Is that a crime?'

'No. It's a bloody temptation,' he growled.

'Stop scowling,' she ordered. 'Superbitch is making her way out for the presentation.'

'*Super*bitch?' He practically choked.

'Yeah.' Courtney grinned up at him. 'Good name for her, isn't it?'

He chuckled darkly. 'You could say that. But you could also say that a certain Ms Courtney Cross runs a close second in the Superbitch stakes.'

Courtney fluttered her eyelashes up at him in mock coyness. 'Who? Li'l ole me? I'm just a poor country girl, trying to keep my head in the company of one very handsome city slicker.'

'Who do you think you're kidding, sweetheart? You

could eat this city slicker for breakfast, then spit me out by lunch-time before getting on your horse and riding out of town without a backward glance.'

'You think so?'

'Honey, I know so. I've always been attracted to strong-willed, independent women with more hide than an elephant, so don't come any of that soft-soap rubbish with me. It won't wash. Now, put on your best Supersiren smile, if you must, and we'll go face Superbitch together.'

So saying, Jack slid an uncompromisingly steely arm around her waist and steered her over to where preparations for the presentation had been carried out on the lawn in front of the members' stand. There was a table which held three magnificent silver and crystal trophies, one large one for the owners, and two smaller replicas for the trainer and jockey, plus a microphone on a stand waiting to service the various speakers.

Oddly, acting the part of Jack's girlfriend during the ceremony didn't amuse Courtney as much this time. She was far too aware of that firm arm around her waist, and the way it kept her glued to his side. It was one thing to admire Jack's macho body from a distance, quite another to feel various muscular parts of it hard up against her, and around her.

There was his long, strong thigh for starters. And the long, strong side of his chest. But mostly that long, strong arm, with its long, strong fingers, whose fingertips began tapping on her hip halfway through the sponsor's speech.

Each tap sent tiny sparks of electricity dancing all through her body, heating her blood and heightening her concern over the ease with which Jack could turn her on. He wasn't even kissing her this time. Just touching her.

No man had ever made her feel what Jack was making her feel, and she wasn't sure if she liked it, or not.

If Katrina hadn't been watching them so closely, she might have pulled away from him and put an end to this highly unusual state of affairs. But awareness of those jealous green eyes fixed on them both had her staying right where she was and smiling adoringly up at him whenever he smiled adoringly down at her.

But once the presentation ceremony was over she excused herself and made a dash for the nearest powder room. She desperately needed a few minutes alone to gather herself. And to think.

She took her time in the cubicle, and was taken aback when she emerged to find Katrina leaning against the vanities, obviously waiting for her. The powder room was strangely empty apart from themselves, yet when she'd first come in the place had been quite crowded.

'I just wanted you to know a few facts of life, little Miss Smug,' Katrina said with cold fury in her voice. 'Jack Falconer does not love you. He'll never love you. So when you're lying in his arms and mooning over how great he is in bed, just remember that it's me he's thinking of when he makes love to you. Not you, honey. Me. Katrina. The love of his life.'

Courtney stared at her. The woman was either a complete nutter or she was telling the truth. Unfortunately, her words had a ring of truth about them.

Courtney did the only thing she could do under the circumstances. She went on the attack.

'Hel-lo? And what planet are *you* from, Ms Seriously Deluded?' she shot back. 'Love of his life? Huh! That's a laugh. Jack has nothing but contempt for you. You're history. So get the hell out of here and go back to your geriatric husband. And when you're lying in his tired old

arms tonight, know that Jack *won't* be thinking about
you. No man thinks of anyone but me when I make love
to them, honey. *I* make sure of that.'

Those already glacial green eyes narrowed to icy slits.
'I'm not the one who's seriously deluded around here.
No doubt Jack has fed you a tissue of lies to suit his own
agenda. But, believe me, Jack is still mad about me.
You're just a stand-in, a cypher, a second-rate substitute.
I could get him back just like *that...*' she snapped her
fingers '...whenever I want.'

'Prove it,' an increasingly angry Courtney challenged.
'Go out there and get him back. Right now. I dare you
to try.'

'Very well. I presume you're seeing Jack tonight, since
you're so inseparable?'

Oops. She would call her bluff, wouldn't she? 'Of
course,' Courtney snapped.

'He'll make some excuse not to see you.'

'Why?'

'Because he'll be with me.'

'I don't believe you.'

'You will.' Her smile was pure malice as she spun on
her high heels, clicked open the lock on the door,
wrenched the door open and left, stepping over the
'Room Being Cleaned' sign she'd obviously placed outside the door to keep people away.

A strangely shaken Courtney stayed in the powder
room, washing her hands for longer than necessary, her
mind revolving. Her well-honed survival instinct warned
her to cut and run where Jack Falconer was concerned,
to have no more to do with him. He was trouble. Big
trouble. And she needed big trouble in her life just now
like she needed a hole in the head.

At the same time, she simply couldn't bear to let that

ghastly creature get away with calling her names. To label her a stand-in and a cypher was bad enough. But second-rate?

There was nothing second-rate about her abilities in bed! Men had lost their heads over her in that regard.

This last thought brought Courtney back to the crux of her earlier worries, which were that maybe this time *she* might be the one who lost her head.

Her mother had always warned about the power that lay within some special men, the power to turn normally intelligent, independent females into simpering idiots and mindless sex slaves.

Courtney appreciated the warning, not just because of the way her own father had effortlessly seduced her strong-willed man-hating mother, but because of the evidence of her own eyes over the years. She'd seen the most hard-nosed tomboy stable girl reduced to mush when a certain type of guy came along. And she'd known quite a few level-headed girls fall pregnant to highly unsuitable charmers.

Why?

They all claimed they'd fallen in love, as if that excused everything. At least her mother hadn't used that excuse. She'd known exactly what had propelled her into her gypsy lover's bed. Courtney didn't believe love had anything to do with those other girls' stupid behaviour, either. It was not love that made them lose all common sense, but a serious case of uncontrollable lust.

Now, *ordinary* oestrogen-based female lust, Courtney was well-acquainted with. Uncontrollable lust, however, was another matter, and not something Courtney thought she would ever encounter, or entertain. Jack was wrong about her having no discipline and self-control. She had a lot of self-control, and exercised it ruthlessly when it came to her sex life. Her relationships with men—such as they were—never got out of hand.

But she'd had a small taste of that other kind of lust now and, whilst it was disturbing, it was also incredibly exciting and unbelievably seductive. How would it feel to surrender herself mindlessly to a man, just once?

Surely she could handle one night of unbridled passion without totally losing it afterwards. Common sense was bound to return, once the cold light of day arrived and the heat of the moment was over.

Courtney stopped washing her hands and stared up at herself in the vanity mirror. The girl who stared back looked no different from the Courtney Cross she was used to. Her eyes often glittered like that. And her cheeks... Well, so what if they were a bit flushed? She'd just had a run-in with Superbitch!

This last thought made up Courtney's mind for her. No way was she going to let that arrogant, smirking woman get her hooks back into Jack again. No way!

With a saucy toss of her head, Courtney whirled on the heels of her black riding boots and deliberately went out to court big trouble.

CHAPTER FIVE

WHEN Courtney emerged into the late-afternoon sunshine once more, Katrina had already drawn Jack over to one side and was whispering frantically to him.

Jack's face was unreadable, but Katrina's was very animated. Almost anguished, at one point.

Courtney couldn't decide if this was a good sign or a bad one. Jack certainly wasn't contributing to this one-sided tête-à-tête. But he wasn't walking away either. Or telling her to get lost. He was listening intently.

As for Katrina's hapless husband, he was at that moment engaged in conversation with one of the club's committee men, blissfully unaware of his darling wife's attempts to seduce Jack practically under his nose.

On sighting Courtney coming across the lawn towards them, Katrina terminated whatever it was she was saying and hurried back to hubby.

'What did *she* want?' Courtney demanded to know.

Jack looked taken aback. 'Excuse me?' he said. 'You don't ask people about their personal conversations.'

'Why not?'

'Because it's rude.'

'Well, *she's* rude. She was *very* rude to me in the ladies' room just now. Called me a cypher and a second-rate substitute. Claimed you were still in love with her and she could get you back just like that.' And she snapped her fingers as Katrina had done.

'I see,' he said coldly.

'Can she, Jack?'

He laughed. 'Never in a million years.'

'That's what I told her. I said she was history. I said all you felt for her was contempt.'

His smile was one of dark satisfaction. 'Good.'

Courtney smiled her own satisfaction. 'As I said before…you're better off without her.'

He didn't answer, his rock-hard gaze following the rapidly departing Mr and Mrs Axelrod.

Consumed with a sudden longing to make this man forget that creature once and for all, Courtney slid her hand into his. 'Jack,' she said softly.

His eyes jerked back to hers. For a few seconds, they looked flat and dead and she thought, *Oh, God, he really does still love her.* But then slowly the life came back into them. His fingers interlinked with hers, then curled over, squeezing tightly.

Her stomach did likewise.

'What are you doing tomorrow?' he asked with seductive softness.

'What are you doing tonight?' she countered.

'Sorry. I have other plans for tonight.'

Her racing heart skittered to a panicky halt.

'Doing what?' she asked almost accusingly.

His smile was sardonic. 'Not what you're thinking. I have some business matters to attend to.'

'On a Saturday night?'

'Yes.'

'You're not going to tell me any more, are you?'

'No.'

'That's cruel. I'm dying of curiosity.'

He smiled. 'And you're going to badger me to death till I tell you.'

'Yes.'

'The fact is, Ms Cross,' he said, lifting her hand to his

lips and kissing the back of it lightly, 'I think I know just the man who'd be an excellent partner for you. But I have to check out a few things first.'

Courtney blinked. 'Are you serious?'

'Would I lie to you?'

Courtney extracted her hand from his. As much as Jack was a distractingly attractive man, and she couldn't wait to discover if his performance in bed matched his reputation, finding the right partner for Crosswinds had to be her first priority. 'Who is he?' she asked. 'Remember, I don't want anyone who's going to interfere in the running of Crosswinds.'

'This fellow will have no interest in interfering.'

'Then who is he? What's his name?'

'I'm not at liberty to say right now.'

'Why not? What's the big secret?'

'No big secret. Just client confidentiality. For now. Meanwhile, don't let Lois go chasing up anyone else. Give my client first crack at it, okay?'

'Suits me. As I said, I don't want any of her horse-mad contacts, no matter how rich they are. I want a big city slicker with absolutely no yen for breeding horses and more money than sense.'

Jack smiled. 'That's exactly what you'll be getting.'

Courtney could hardly believe her luck. Both her problems solved at once. Her debts. Plus her rather disturbing desire for this man.

She'd been wondering how she could confine any fling with Jack to one time only if she stayed down here in Sydney for a whole week. Jack wasn't the sort of man who would let her run the show as she usually did. If he was as passionate and powerful a lover as he was a kisser, then he'd be the one directing the action, and deciding when enough was enough.

Which was partly the point, of course.

Courtney wanted to feel what it would be like, being made love to by a dominating and possibly demanding man. She didn't, however, want to become addicted to the experience. She had no doubt Jack intended to seduce her tomorrow, but hopefully, by Monday, she could escape back to the normality of home, never to see him again. After all, business contracts were handled by electronic mail these days, as were cash transfers. There would be no need for any further personal contact. Bill could handle the details, and any follow-up business.

She beamed up at him. 'Wait till I tell Lois. She's going to be so pleased.'

'Tell me what?'

Courtney swung round to find a happy Lois standing there, clasping her trophy. Jack's was still on the table.

'Jack thinks he knows just the right sucker to save Crosswinds.'

'Partner,' Jack corrected drily. 'Not sucker.'

'*Silent* partner,' Courtney countered. 'He won't open his mouth, just his wallet. Isn't that right, Jack?'

'Not quite. He's no fool, Courtney. He'll want to know exactly what he's getting himself into. After a recent, rather unfortunate experience he had, he'll want me to go up to Crosswinds and check everything out firsthand. There *are* tax concessions for investments in thoroughbred breeding, but I'm going to have to assure my client that Crosswinds is a going concern with potential for a steady future income and return on his investment.'

'Oh… How long would you have to stay?'

'I'll need a few days to be totally satisfied,' he confirmed. 'You did say it was a large concern. I'll also need to speak to your accountant and see the books. If you haven't any other business to do here in Sydney, we could drive up there together tomorrow.'

'Well, I…er…' Courtney wasn't usually tongue-tied, but Jack's suggestion had totally routed her own nice safe plan which would prevent any chance of any sexual addiction or, heaven forbid, an emotional involvement.

Courtney had no intention of ever succumbing to either. But she had wanted to let her hair down, so to speak, just this once.

Now, any such experience was out of the question. No way would Courtney invite Jack into her bedroom at Crosswinds and risk any of her staff finding out. It was hard enough to maintain their respect as their boss with her being female and attractive and only twenty-five. Impossible if they thought she was an easy lay.

Courtney had never had sex with any of the men working at Crosswinds. Well…not since her first time, five years before. But Larry had been leaving the next day, so the risk hadn't been great. And she hadn't been the boss back then.

'Fine,' she said, irritated by this turn of events.

'I thought you were out of the investment brokerage business, Jack,' Lois remarked.

Lois wasn't sure what was going on between these two, but something was up. She wasn't blind. She'd seen that kiss in the stands. It hadn't been an impromptu peck on the cheek, either. It had been a full-blooded, open-mouthed, French kiss. Then, at the presentation, they'd been all over each other like a rash.

Jack obviously had more on his mind than just finding Courtney a business partner. His intention of staying at Crosswinds until he was *totally satisfied* could be construed two ways.

'This chap is by way of being a personal friend of

mine,' Jack attempted to explain, and Lois's excellent antenna for male deception twanged. She hoped there really *was* a potential partner, and this wasn't some plan for a rebound or revenge affair. Lois had seen Jack with Katrina on many occasions and she knew just how wrapped in her he'd been. It seemed far too coincidental that this sudden passion for Courtney had come about on the very day Jack's ex had been around.

'Why doesn't he want his identity known?' she challenged, scepticism in her voice.

'He likes to play a close hand. He'll be up front with Courtney, if and when he goes ahead with the partnership. You have my word.'

'That's good,' Lois said.

Lois didn't really think Jack was the type to rip Courtney off in any money sense. As far as their personal relationship was concerned…well, she supposed Courtney could look after herself in that regard. Hilary might have been a man-hater, but her daughter was rumoured to be a real man-eater. The horseworld grapevine was second to none, and men invariably talked. There'd been this horse-breaker a few years back. And a rep who sold horse vitamins. And a chap who drove for a horse transport company. And they were only the ones Lois had heard about.

Maybe the person she should be worrying about was Jack…

CHAPTER SIX

SUNDAY dawned crisp and clear, with the promise of another warm winter's day. Courtney, as befitted her habit of years, was up at first light. Lois had still preceded her by a couple of hours, overseeing her charges on the training track well before the sun's first rays peeped over the horizon. Her horses were back in their mucked-out stables long before most Sydneysiders opened their Sunday morning papers.

Lois still insisted on cooking Courtney breakfast, treating them both to bacon and eggs and lashings of toast and brewed coffee, serving all of it up on the round wooden table which dominated the homey kitchen in her red-roofed, three-bedroomed, fifties-style brick-veneer house. She'd inherited it—plus the stables—from her horse trainer father, who'd died of a stroke after one of his charges had come back with a positive swab and his licence had been taken away from him. Her mother had passed away a few years before or she, too, would have died of shame, Lois believed.

Lois, thirtyish at the time and in the throes of divorce, had taken up the challenge of making a success of the career she'd always wanted but which her mother had talked her out of in favour of marriage to a Macquarie Street specialist with two huge cars and a house on the harbour. All he'd needed to complete his perfect lifestyle was a beautiful wife and two beautiful children.

Lois hadn't been able to have any children, however, which was one of the reasons her marriage had failed.

That, along with the loneliness and boredom of being a doctor's wife. Her horses were now her children, which perhaps explained why they could never do any wrong in her eyes. No matter what fault they had—even being too slow—she was always sure she could fix it. The funny thing was, often enough she could.

'Sleep well?' Lois remarked over their second cup.

The girl looked tired, she thought. Though still beautiful. How was it that when you were only twenty-five dark circles under your eyes looked sexy, but once you passed forty you just looked wrecked?

'Fine,' Courtney lied. She'd tossed and turned for most of the night, unable to get out of her mind that Jack might have lied to her, that he was, at that very moment, making mad, passionate love to the awful but stunningly gorgeous Katrina.

Her emotions had kept alternating between anger and jealousy, though who exactly she was most angry with she wasn't sure. She still wasn't. Probably Jack, for even falling in love with such a creature in the first place. My God, didn't he have any taste? The woman was a witch, a manipulative, gold-digging, heartless witch.

Who was probably brilliant in bed.

More than brilliant.

Bad.

Men liked women to be bad in bed. They liked it a lot. Courtney knew that for a fact.

'It's Jack, isn't it?' Lois said abruptly.

Courtney's darkly bruised eyes whipped up from where she'd been staring blankly down at her plate. 'What?'

'Jack Falconer. You fancy him.'

Courtney shrugged. 'Who wouldn't?'

'I don't. He's not my type at all.'

Surprise that Lois even *had* a type must have shown in her face, for Lois laughed.

'You think I don't have a sex life?'

'I…I guess I never really thought about it at all.'

'Typical. The young think sex is only for the young.'

'No, I don't,' Courtney denied. 'I just thought you were totally wrapped up in your horses and didn't want or need a man in your life. Mum said you were divorced, and I guess I jumped to conclusions. The *wrong* conclusions, I see,' she added, feeling both curious and intrigued by this woman who had been on the fringes of her life for many years but whom she'd never bothered to really get to know. Yet she liked her. She liked her a lot. 'So what *is* your type, Lois? Tell me.'

'Hard to describe, exactly. But I know it when I see it. He's usually of average height. I don't like men to tower over me. Nicely built without being muscle-bound. Elegant in his movements. A good rider,' she said, her smile wicked. 'And with dark eyes. I adore dark eyes.'

'How old?'

'Age is immaterial. I've had lovers in their twenties and in their fifties.'

'And where do you find these men?' Courtney knew how hard it was to have a relationship with a man when you worked with horses. It was a seven-day-a-week job.

'I hire them.'

Courtney tried not to look shocked, and almost managed. 'You…hire…them,' she said slowly, her mind whirling. 'As in…how? From an escort agency?'

Lois chuckled. 'Lord, no. I mean I hire them to work for me. You must know how often grooms come and go in this business. When I'm interviewing new staff, if I see a fellow who appeals to me physically, I hire him.'

'Good grief. And does he…um…they…um…always come across?'

'Most of the time. I'm the boss, after all.'

'Wow!'

'You're not too shocked?'

'No! Heavens, no. But don't these men…um…talk?'

Lois shrugged. 'Not often. They know what side their bed is buttered on. To be honest, I'd prefer a permanent relationship, but not many men can handle a woman as strong as myself on a day-to-day basis.'

'I know what you mean.'

'What about you, Courtney? Will you be looking to get married one day?'

'Never.' She'd never met one single married man who didn't want to be the boss of his wife. Not one. And she knew she could never handle that.

'What about children? Don't you want children?'

Courtney had always pushed the issue of children to the back of her mind. 'I'll probably have a child one day. I'd like someone to leave Crosswinds to. But I don't have to be married for that. And I don't see any rush. I'm only twenty-five.'

'True. But the years have a habit of slipping away from you. You wouldn't want to wake up one day and find out it's too late.'

The telephone began ringing.

'Excuse me a moment,' Lois said. 'It's probably an owner. Sunday is visiting day.'

She swivelled round in her chair and reached for the mobile phone which was resting on the kitchen counter. She pressed the button and swept it up to her ear.

'Lois Wymouth speaking,' she said sweetly. 'Well, if it isn't Jack Falconer!'

Courtney stiffened in her chair.

'You're up bright and early. Did our mystery investor come to the party…? Wonderful…! He doesn't…? God, talk about super-secretive… She's upstairs… I'll go and get her for you…'

She cupped her hand firmly over the phone. 'Looks like you have your sucker. But he still wants to keep his ID a secret till he signs on the dotted line. Anyway, lover-boy wants to talk to you personally. Would you like to take the call somewhere more private?' she whispered.

'Just give me the phone, Lois. Nothing of that kind will be going on between me and Jack now that I'm doing business with him. Unlike some people, I don't mix business and pleasure.'

'Oooh. That's power talking for you. But will you be able to sustain your good intentions when you have Jack all to yourself up in that big old house for a few days *and* nights? I don't see him playing gentleman for that long. Not when he fancies you as much as you fancy him. And he does. I do have eyes, girl.'

Courtney had been worrying about exactly the same thing herself. 'I'll have Biggs sleep on my bed.'

'That old mongrel? Your stable cat is a better guard dog than him.'

'Maybe. But Biggs looks fiercer.'

'Well, take my advice and get in a good supply of condoms. Don't want any unexpected little filly or colt arriving next year, do we?'

'As if I'd ever let myself accidentally get pregnant to any man. Don't you think I learnt anything from my mother? Now *give* me the darned phone!'

Lois sighed, and handed it over. Courtney rose and walked into the lounge-room, away from prying ears. 'Jack! Lois said you have some good news for me.'

'I surely do. It's all systems go. My client is happy to

invest the four million in Crosswinds you need, provided everything is shipshape.'

Courtney frowned. 'Er…what does he mean by shipshape? I did explain to you the place is looking a bit run-down. That's why I wanted the four million instead of the three I already owe the bank.'

'I'm not talking about surface appearances. I'm talking about the land itself and the quality of your stock. The brood mares and the stallions you have standing at stud. Especially the latter.'

'We have three stallions at stud, two older well-formed stallions and one exciting new prospect.'

'Goldplated,' he said before she could.

'You *know* about him?'

'I looked him up last night. He's impeccably bred, the full brother to a Golden Slipper winner. He never started in a race after an accident on the training track, though he had won two well-documented trials in brilliant fashion. He stood his first and only season at a stud in Victoria, with an amazing fertility strike-rate of one hundred per cent. Which raises the question of why did they sell him?'

'That's easily answered. That stud stands his full brother as well, the Golden Slipper winner. They felt it wasn't commercially sensible to keep two stallions of exactly the same blood lines. But they were wanting to use Goldplated just once on some of their own mares before they let him go. I think you'll find he didn't service any outside mares.'

'They sold him at a bargain basement price.'

'That's because he's still a risk. It'll be two more years before his first crop reaches the track. A lot can happen between now and then.'

'I hope he's insured,' Jack said.

'Do I look like a fool?' Courtney thanked God for Bill, or she would have.

'Right, well, I'll want to know exactly how many mares Goldplated is booked to cover this season, how much you currently charge for his services, and how much you might be able to charge in the years to come, if his progeny start winning good races. This is obviously a long-term investment and my client will want to know what Crosswinds' prospects are, long-term.'

Courtney frowned. 'You've certainly done your research.'

'Amazing what you find out on the internet.'

'Is that what you were doing last night? Finding out what you could about breeding racehorses?'

'Partly.'

Courtney pulled a face. He sure liked to play his cards close to his chest. 'I see. Well, Sarah will be able to give you all the facts and figures on all our brood mares and stallions.' She'd already decided to turn Jack over to as many other people as she could during his stay at Crosswinds. 'Sarah's the office manager at Crosswinds. She's been there for yonks and probably knows more about those things than I do.'

Which was just so much bullardust. There wasn't anyone at Crosswinds who knew more about the horses there than Courtney.

'When can you be ready to leave?' Jack asked. 'I was thinking of a ten o'clock start. Would that be too early for you?'

Courtney glanced at the chiming clock in the corner of the lounge-room. It was ten to nine. She was already up, showered, dressed and breakfasted. Packing would take all of five minutes.

'I'm ready now,' she said, and he laughed.

'I guess I'm used to a different type of female. Katrina needed at least a day's notice of intent to go anywhere.'

Courtney thought of Katrina's perfect hair and exquisitely made-up face. No doubt the rest of her required as much time-consuming pampering. Her clothes selection for each occasion probably took hours. And she'd have to race out and buy something new if she didn't have *just* the right thing.

'Speaking of Katrina,' Courtney couldn't resist saying, 'did she happen to accidentally show up at your place last night?'

'No,' he said without hesitation. 'She did not. Happy now?' he added, a cool amusement in his voice.

Courtney realised she'd just made her first mistake, if she wanted to keep this man at arm's length. 'Just checking to make sure you weren't too exhausted to drive all day,' she said drily.

'It's only about six hours to the Upper Hunter Valley. Longer if we stop. Which we will, of course.'

'Oh?'

'For lunch.'

Reasons for stopping other than for lunch had flashed into Courtney's mind.

'I'll bring a picnic,' he said.

The vision of them lying together on a rug on some sun-drenched riverbank was not conducive to Courtney's rapidly disintegrating peace of mind.

'Please don't do that,' she said sharply.

'Why not?'

She decided to nip things in the bud.

'This is a business trip, Jack, not some romantic getaway. I'm sorry if I gave you the wrong idea yesterday. I *am* very attracted to you, I admit. But I don't mix business with pleasure, and that's final.'

'That's telling me straight, isn't it?'

'It's better to be up front. Saves trouble later on.'

'What kind of trouble are you referring to?'

'Having to handle men who think I'm going to be a push-over in my business dealings with them just because I'm sleeping with them.'

'And that's happened to you in the past?'

'In a fashion.' That vitamin rep had expected her to buy swags of his stuff, just because she'd spent one wretched weekend away with him.

'Does it occur to you that all the power in this case is on your side?' Jack said drily. 'Sleeping with me might get me to overlook any shortcomings in Crosswinds.'

'I don't believe that for a moment.'

'Why not?'

'Because any man who paid back all his partner's debts out of his own purse when he didn't have to is not going to play deceitful with a client.'

'There's always the first time,' he said wryly.

'No, Jack. That's not you.'

'Not me,' he repeated slowly. 'I doubt you know the real me, Courtney.'

'I have a pretty good idea. I'm quite a good judge of character. I have every confidence that you won't put the hard word on me, if I ask you not to. But if you're ever tempted, I'll have Biggs by my side.'

'Who the hell is Biggs? Some kind of bodyguard?'

'My trusty guard dog. He's a cattle dog cross. He comes with me everywhere.' A slight exaggeration. Mr Biggs, who was rising ten, spent most of his days snoozing on the swing seat on the front veranda. Only occasionally did he wander around the farm with her nowadays. And he *never* went in the ute with her any more, ever since she'd run into a ditch the previous year and he'd been thrown out of the passenger window, landing in a freshly deposited cow-pat. His dignity had been seriously offended.

'Thanks for telling me,' Jack said ruefully.

'I thought it only fair to warn you.'

'In that case, it's only fair that I warn you in return.'

Courtney stiffened. 'About what?'

'I don't take orders very well.'

'Meaning?'

'Just that. See you at ten. *With* a picnic basket.' And he hung up.

CHAPTER SEVEN

'WOULD you like to have a turn behind the wheel?' Jack asked an hour into the trip. They had not long crossed the Mooney Mooney bridge, and were heading north on the F3 freeway which connected Sydney to Newcastle. Traffic was light, compared to what was heading south towards Sydney.

Courtney shot Jack a surprised glance. When he'd first pulled up outside Lois's place in a red sports convertible with the top down and a personalised number plate— JF2000—on it, she'd been agape with shock. When she'd questioned how he could afford to even *insure* such a car, he'd shrugged and said that he'd bought it to celebrate the new millennium. And what the heck? You only lived once.

Courtney's sentiments exactly. She adored sports cars. Always had. She was sure she would adore driving one, but had never had the chance. Till now.

'You mean it?' she asked, her heart thundering.

To show her he did, he immediately pulled over to the side of the road, leaving the powerful engine growling impatiently whilst he jumped out and strode round the low, sleek front of the car.

Courtney ogled him every step of the way, thinking he looked even more hunky in casual clothes than he did in a suit. His long legs, narrow hips and compact butt were just made for jeans, and his big chest and broad shoulders impressively filled out his navy blue pullover. He would look damned good in the buff, she couldn't help thinking.

'Well, what are you still sitting there for, girl?' he chided when he yanked open her door. 'Hop to it.'

Courtney snapped out of her lust-filled reverie, leapt out and raced round before he could change his mind, telling herself that if she couldn't enjoy his body then she was darned well going to enjoy his car!

'Don't forget there's a one-ten speed limit on this road,' Jack warned when she roared off.

'Do you think they'd book me at one-twenty?'

'Yes. So stick to one-fifteen. Max.'

'Okay, boss.' She flashed him a happy grin.

'That'll be the day,' he muttered, and Courtney laughed.

The next hour was thrilling! So much better than driving the ute. Courtney hummed happily as she sped along the expressway with the wind in her face and her ponytail streaming out behind.

'This must be what it felt like riding Big Brutus down the straight yesterday,' she shouted at one stage. 'Fan-bloody-tastic!'

The turn-off for the New England highway came up all too quickly, with Jack asking her to pull over shortly afterwards.

'Can't trust you to slow down for all the little towns we go through on this road,' Jack commented once he was behind the wheel again. 'I can see you're a speed freak.'

'I am,' she said, nodding agreement. 'I just love anything fast. Always have.'

'And what else do you love?' he asked, his sexy blue eyes slanting her a seductive glance.

Courtney's stomach curled over, making her realise that driving Jack's car had undermined her defences where he was concerned. It was high time to get herself

under control again. In a few short hours they would be
at Crosswinds and this would never do, having her in-
sides flip over every time he looked at her.

'I love being behind the wheel,' she said firmly, 'in
everything I do.'

'That can be exhausting. Aren't there ever times when
you just want to lie back, relax and let someone else be
responsible for things?'

She glared over at him. Was he a damned mind-reader?

'Turn in here,' she ordered abruptly, and noted with
triumph that he did as he was told. Sometimes.

It was a rest area in the middle of nowhere. There
wasn't any babbling brook. Or any softly grassed bank.
Just a small clearing carved into the scrubby roadside
bush and a few straggly trees left to provide shade for a
couple of picnic tables and benches.

'Why do you want to stop here?' Jack asked, scowling.

'I'm hungry. I thought this would be a good spot for
our picnic lunch.'

The corner of his wide, firm mouth lifted in a smile of
considerable irony. 'As good as any,' he agreed, 'under
the circumstances.'

Courtney almost regretted her decision to lunch there
when she saw Jack's truly beautiful picnic box and its
simply delicious contents. Fortunately, he had a checked
tablecloth which covered the rickety table.

'You shouldn't have gone to all this trouble,' she
chided as he set everything out on the cloth.

'No trouble at all. I rang and ordered it from the local
deli after my call to you this morning, then picked it up
on my way.'

Courtney gazed at the delicious selection of cold
meats, salads, cheeses and breads. There was even a
chilled half-bottle of white wine along with two classy-

looking glasses. 'It must have been very expensive,' she said with a frown.

'Reasonably. But please don't fuss. Just enjoy. Think of it as your commission for tipping me Big Brutus. Believe me when I say I still have plenty of change left from my winnings.'

To continue complaining would have been ungracious in the extreme, so Courtney shrugged and tucked in.

Having given in, she ate her fair share and drank most of the wine, which went straight to her head.

'Brother!' she exclaimed when she felt her head begin to spin. 'What percentage alcohol is in this?' She picked up the bottle and read that it was twelve per cent. 'Pretty potent drop. You trying to get me tipsy?'

'If I was, I'd have bought a whole bottle.'

'True,' she conceded.

'Would it make any difference? Are you a sure thing when you're tipsy?'

'Not too often.'

'But sometimes?' He looked hopeful.

'I hope you haven't come on this jaunt hoping I would be.'

'No.'

'You think you can talk me into it, is that it?'

'But of course. I wouldn't be a normal red-blooded heterosexual male if I didn't.'

Exasperation with him brought heat to her face. 'I thought I told you that's not on!'

Jack remained annoyingly cool. And terrifyingly confident. 'I know what you told me. But, as I said, I don't take orders. And your reasons for not sleeping with me don't wash, Courtney. You're not doing business with me personally. You're doing it with my client.'

'Other people won't see it like that,' she argued.

'There's absolutely no need for anyone at Crosswinds to know, if that's what you're afraid of. I can be very discreet. What happens behind closed bedroom doors is our business only. Though, to tell the truth, I'd prefer an open relationship with you. But if you insist on secrecy, then I won't give the game away.'

His eyes met hers and held them effortlessly.

Her whole world tipped sidewards, then whirled. She was like a spinning top that he'd suddenly set in motion—that he would always be able to set in motion with the touch of his hand or, as now, with that devilish gleam in his eye.

A scary thought. But oh…so thrilling. More thrilling than driving his car. More thrilling than anything she'd ever known.

She thanked God the wide wooden table lay between them or she'd drag his deliciously macho mouth onto hers right then and there, and Lord knew what would happen then. Passing traffic might start running off the road on spotting them making love on the table, with picnic things scattered everywhere!

'I'll think about it,' she said abruptly, and reefed her eyes away to start stacking up the empty containers.

She could feel his eyes still on her but she simply refused to look back at him, refused to let him see how much power he already had over her.

'You do that,' he drawled, then began to help.

CHAPTER EIGHT

THEY didn't stop again, or really talk again; the next few hours were agonisingly long for Courtney. Jack commented once on the scenic countryside, and complained occasionally over some fool's driving, usually a truck driver. He also put the radio on and sang softly along with a few songs, but they were only minor distractions for her increasingly panicky thoughts.

I'm a goner, she finally accepted a few minutes away from their turn-off. Come tonight, I'm going to end up in bed with Jack Falconer. No point in fighting it any longer.

Better to go willingly, she decided, than to act like Biggs when he had to go to the vet.

She almost burst out laughing at the image of herself with a lead around her throat, being dragged into Jack's bedroom, her heels digging into the polished wooden floor while she whimpered in fear.

As it was, an amused little giggle escaped.

No, that was not her. She was not a coward. Or a victim. She made the rules in her sex life. She would stick to those rules again tonight, and if Jack wanted to try anything other than her usual she would tell him that didn't work for her and he could just like what she was offering, or lump it!

She had no doubt he would like it. Every man she'd ever known had, and had come begging for more.

'Want to share the source of your return to good humour?' Jack asked.

'No,' she returned blithely. 'Take the next turn on the left.'

'Queenswood, ten kilometres,' he read on the sign as he turned. 'How far is your place from there?'

'About fifteen kilometres the other side of town. But I'd like to stop in Queenswood, if you don't mind. I've got a couple of things to pick up. If there's anything you need at the shops, I suggest you get it now. You don't want to be running back and forth for minor provisions. The road to Crosswinds is not the best. The tar gives way to dirt pretty quickly, and the surface is very rutted at the moment after all the rain we've had this last winter.'

'Too much rain?'

She shrugged. 'A lot of rain in winter is a double-edged sword. You do get good grass in the spring but it drowned some of the oats we planted. Still, I'm not complaining. We can always plant some more.'

'You know, you have an optimistic spirit. I like that.'

'Not as optimistic as Lois. That woman cracks me up sometimes.'

'Is that another warning about Big Brutus's chances in the Melbourne Cup?'

'No! Lord, no! I wasn't even thinking about Big Brutus.'

'What were you thinking about, then?'

'Nothing specific.' But she had been. She'd been thinking of Lois having the hide to employ men she fancied, then coercing them into bed with her because she was the boss. Courtney had always thought herself bold, but Lois left her for dead.

At least Jack *wanted* to go to bed with her. He had no ulterior motive or secret agenda. For him, it was simply a matter of sex.

And that was how she was determined to look at tonight. Simply as a matter of sex. No different from any of the other encounters she'd had with men in the past.

'Ah, here we are,' she said, feeling marginally better.

Queenswood was typical of most Australian towns, with a very wide main street lined by shops, a nice little park on entry and exit, a pub on one corner, a post office on another and the town hall in the centre, usually sporting a clock tower.

Queenswood's clock told Courtney it was five past four. Jack had made very good time, even without going over the speed limit.

'Just park anywhere there in the middle,' she told him. 'There's plenty of spaces. Not too many people in town at this hour on a Sunday afternoon. All the shops will be closed by now, except for the supermarket and the chemist. You need anything?'

'No. I don't think so.'

'Fine. Won't be long.'

Courtney bowled into the chemist shop with every intention of buying a packet of condoms. It wouldn't have been the first time. But the chemist's wife, Maggie, was serving at the counter and she was the town's resident gossip. So Courtney picked up the first thing that came to hand—a can of muskily perfumed deodorant—paid for it quickly, and left, after which she dashed into the supermarket.

Fortunately, the cashier was a gum-chewing magazine-reading adolescent girl whom Courtney didn't recognise and who hardly stopped reading when Courtney went through with her purchase.

As she hurried out, Courtney popped the box of condoms inside the opaque paper bag containing the deodorant, secretly glad there weren't too many people around to stare at her getting into a red sports car driven by a very handsome stranger. Gossip was the bane of country life, and discretion was necessary if you cared what other people thought.

Till recently, Courtney hadn't given a damn what people thought of her. Other than her mother, that was. But her mother was gone now and the responsibility for Crosswinds lay on her shoulders and hers alone. She *had* to care what some people thought, whether she liked it or not.

Jack had climbed out of the car whilst she was gone and was leaning with his back against his door, his arms folded and his ankles crossed. His head was tipped back slightly, his eyes were shut and he was soaking in the last of the afternoon sun. He looked totally relaxed and totally irresistible to Courtney.

She couldn't stop her eyes running over him in a decidedly lascivious fashion, lingering on the bulge in his jeans. Lord, now that was impressive. *Very* impressive.

Her eyes finally lifted to find that his eyelids had done likewise during her highly intimate perusal. 'I see you've been thinking about it,' he drawled.

She swallowed, but kept her eyes steady. Don't let him get cocky. Don't let him be sure of you.

Her small smile was just enough to make him stand up straight, his body language showing a measure of frustration. His lower body too, if she wasn't mistaken.

'As I said yesterday,' he muttered, yanking open his car door, and hiding his arousal from her, 'you run a close second in the Superbitch stakes, Courtney Cross.'

'I never run second in anything,' she retorted, stung by his putting her in the same breath as that calculating cold-blooded cow. 'No crime in a girl looking. But I did warn you, Jack. I don't mix business with pleasure. You should have believed me.'

'I'm beginning to appreciate that fact.'

'You can't win them all, you know.'

'Just get in the car, damn you.'

'Fine!'

They climbed in and banged their car doors simultaneously. Courtney threw her package at her feet, sorry that she'd even bothered to buy the darned things now. All that rampant desire she'd been feeling for Jack had well and truly disintegrated with their spat. Which was just as well, since she'd just told the man sex was definitely not on.

Jack shot out of his parking spot like a spurred quarter-horse, racing up the main street and out of town. When he hit the dirt road his back wheels slewed round, throwing up a cloud of dust which would have covered Lake Eyre.

'Careful,' Courtney bit out. 'I ended up in a ditch last year driving too fast along this road.'

'Pity you didn't break your beautiful neck in the process.'

Courtney was torn between feeling offended and complimented. She hadn't had her neck described as beautiful before. Probably because it wasn't, she decided. It was too darned long.

'Flattery will get you everywhere,' she snapped.

'Will it, now?'

His blue eyes glittered harshly as they flicked over her body, encased that day in blue jeans and a red and blue checked flannel shirt. With her hair up in a ponytail and no make-up on, Courtney knew she was as far removed from the glamorous and perfectly groomed Katrina as a woman could be. But Jack was still looking at her with the most corruptingly intense hunger.

'In that case you have beautiful eyes as well. A beautiful mouth, beautiful legs, beautiful breasts, and, oh, yes, a really beautiful backside. So how far has that got me?' he mocked. 'Through your bedroom door yet? Or do I need to mention your refreshing personality, your feisty spirit, your earthy sensuality and your wicked sense of humour?'

Courtney couldn't help it. She burst out laughing.

He grinned also and, thankfully, slowed down to a less neck-risking speed. She really did want to get home in one piece.

'You lied to me,' he said, but with a smile.

'About what?'

'About flattery getting me everywhere. It hasn't made the slightest bit of difference, has it?'

'No.'

'And I suppose they aren't condoms in that packet down there, as I was stupidly hoping?'

'Sorry, just deodorant for me and some headache tablets for Agnes,' she said with a perfectly straight face.

'Pity.'

'Them's the breaks.'

'That was your last chance to give in gracefully. From now on it's war, where all sorts of dirty tactics will be employed.'

'Such as?'

'You don't expect me to telegraph my punches, do you? That's not how the game is played.'

'War is not a game.'

'It can be. I played war games a lot as a kid. And I know all the right moves.'

'I'm sure you do,' she said ruefully.

'Them kind of moves, too,' he agreed with a devilish waggle of his brows. 'I've had loads of practice.'

'Start young, did you?'

'Fourteen, or thereabouts.'

'Disgusting.'

'I'll bet you weren't far behind, you little hypocrite. Country girls are notorious for being sexually active young. Something to do with seeing all those animal matings from an early age. Sex holds no mystery.'

'You're right there. Sex certainly held no mysteries for me, which is why I was twenty before I bothered.'

He threw her a startled look.

'It's true. Before then I wouldn't even kiss a boy. If anything, seeing stallions servicing mares all the time made me even more determined not to succumb to such a male-orientated activity. It's not pretty to watch, you know. Or sexy. The mare is tied up and quite often reluctant. But she has no choice. The stallion is brought in and he mounts her whether she likes it or not. Virgin mares whinny with the pain. Others freeze with shock.'

'But surely not all mares react like that.'

'No. There are born sluts, even in mares. Or so my mother used to say.'

Jack frowned. 'Surely *you* don't think that, do you? That a female is a born slut if she enjoys sex?'

'Not any more I don't. But I did for a long while. I hated the idea of a man on top of me, forcing part of his body into mine. I couldn't understand how it could be pleasurable, let alone bearable.'

'But you obviously don't think that now,' he said, still sounding a bit shocked.

'No. I don't think that now. Thanks to Larry.'

'Larry,' he repeated thoughtfully. 'Larry who?'

'Larry Mason. He was a horse-breaker. Specialised in difficult fillies.'

'Very funny. Were you in love with him?'

She laughed. 'Good Lord, no. But he was very attractive in a John Wayne sort of way.'

'And?'

'And I fancied him rotten.'

'And?'

Suddenly it all came back to her, like a slow-motion movie. She'd gone down to the far feed shed for something and walked in on Larry and one of the stable girls, having sex. Larry had been lying across some bales of straw and the girl had been sitting astride him, totally unaware of her surroundings as she'd risen and fallen on her lover's body, her eyes tightly shut, moaning cries escaping her wide open mouth. She hadn't seen Courtney standing there, frozen but fascinated.

Larry had, however. He'd even winked at her. She'd watched for a full five minutes before running away.

She hadn't told anyone what she'd seen, but after that, whenever she'd run into Larry, he'd stare at her and she'd go hot all over. She'd thought about him constantly, had dreamt of him at night: dreamt of sitting astride him as that girl had done. Dreamt of clutching his shoulders and riding him till she too cried out with the kind of orgasm she'd witnessed that afternoon.

Courtney had read all about orgasms. She just hadn't ever wanted one before.

But after that she had. With Larry.

Yet she hadn't dared approach him, fearing her mother might find out. But then she'd heard Larry was leaving the next day, going to work at a stud in South Australia. That had been her chance. And she'd taken it, dredging up the courage to go to him and tell him what she wanted, even whilst she'd been shaking inside.

That night it had been *her* in the far shed with him, not that stable girl. Her being shown how to do what she'd seen, and more. Much more. Larry liked assertive women, as it had turned out. He liked them being on top. He liked being made love to by the female.

Courtney had liked it too. Because she'd been in control. There'd been no question of male domination. Or of losing her head. The next time she'd met a man she fancied, she'd known exactly what to do. Not that there'd been all that many. Three or four over five years. Hardly a harem.

'You must have fancied this Larry one hell of a lot,' Jack persisted, 'if he got past all your obvious defences. Either that or he was the best seducer since Casanova. Which was it?'

Courtney suddenly realised Jack's questions had become very intimate indeed.

Time to terminate this conversation!

'I fancied him one hell of a lot,' she said. 'Watch this next corner. This is where I ran off the road.'

Jack's car took the corner as if it was on rails, and in a way it was, the deep, rain-worn ruts keeping all four wheels securely within their walls. But when the low-slung bottom of the car scraped the top off the hump of dirt in the middle, Jack groaned.

'I can see why people have four-wheel drives out here,' he grumbled.

'It'll be better once the council brings in the grader. They do that a couple of times a year.'

'You should get on their backs to do more. Put some road base down or something. This is appalling.'

'This is the country, Jack, not the city.'

'Still...'

Always sensitive to male criticism, Courtney was now on the alert for more, their arrival at the official entrance into Crosswinds making her smother a groan as she suddenly saw it through Jack's eyes.

The once proud iron archway, which had the word 'Crosswinds' emblazoned across it, was rusty, as was the cut-out drum sitting on a fence post, which served as their mailbox. Not an auspicious entrance for a property looking for an investor.

Courtney waited for Jack to make a detrimental comment but he didn't. He just drove through the open gateway without saying a word.

At least the driveway up to the house was gravel, she thought, and not rutted or potholed. The tall poplars on either side looked impressive, too, though the trees hadn't sprouted their leaves yet. Which was a pity. Their greenery would have distracted from the fences behind, whose greying paint seemed to have disintegrated further in the short time she'd been away.

Still, the land beyond the peeling fences did look good, the lushly grassed paddocks and green hills beyond presenting a panoramic picture of surface prosperity. Peaceful mares grazed in yards on the left, whilst healthy-looking yearlings frolicked on the right. The various barns and buildings in the distance didn't look as shabby as they would up close.

Hopefully, Jack's first impressions overall would be good. After all, she'd warned him about the recent lack of money to attend to what were really superficial things. He was the one who'd said it was the quality of the land and stock that mattered.

Jack continued up the winding driveway at a sedate pace, his head swivelling left and right, his intelligent eyes drinking it all in.

When his head stopped swivelling and his eyes stared straight ahead, Courtney's own gaze followed.

Satisfaction filled her soul at the sight that had trans-fixed him. Her home, perched on the hill at the far end of the driveway, looking magnificent.

'What a fantastic old house,' Jack said warmly.

'I'm so glad you think so.'

She smiled as her eyes moved lovingly over the house's stately grandeur, shown to advantage under the golden rays of the setting sun. The grey iron roof shone, and the white iron-lace balustrades which ran round the upstairs veranda sparkled. Any lack of recent painting certainly didn't show in the flattering afternoon light.

'My great great-grandfather built it back in 1852, when he first bought the land and started up the stud. He was a merchant from Scotland and quite wealthy. The walls are made out of a local sandstone and all the woodwork is Australian cedar. The lead light panels in the doors and windows were made in Melbourne and transported up by bullock wagons. The marble tiles in the front hallway were shipped out from Devon and the brass light fittings were manufactured somewhere in the north of England. I can't remember where exactly. He filled the whole house with wonderful European furniture, but unfortu-nately we only have a few pieces left.'

'That's a shame.'

'You can say that again. I wouldn't have come begging to Sydney if I'd still had them. I'd have just auctioned off the damned lot and paid off my debts. But Mum beat me to it. Over the years, every time she wanted to buy a brood mare she couldn't afford, she sold off a piece of furniture and replaced it with a cheap reproduction. As it is, all we have left is an ancient four-poster bed which stayed because it couldn't be moved out of the room without being totally taken apart.'

'*We?*' Jack probed. 'I thought you were an only child.'

'I was. I'm talking about me and Agnes.'

'The housekeeper?'

'I shouldn't have called her that. She's much more than a housekeeper. She's another reason why I'll do everything in my power to keep Crosswinds a going concern. She'd be lost if she ever had to move out and find somewhere else to live. The house is her life. And me too, I guess. We have a bit of a love-hate relationship at times, me and Agnes.'

'How old is she?'

'I have no idea. She's strangely coy about her age, but she looks about sixty. Sixty-five, maybe. She's one of those thin, wiry women who's always on the go. Indefatigable, my mother used to call her.'

'She sounds a character.'

'She is. And a sweetie underneath her brusque exterior. Tell her you like her cooking and she'll be your slave for life. Ah, there she is, waiting for us on the front veranda. I rang her this morning after you called, to let her know we'd be home in time for dinner.'

'She looks closer to seventy to me,' Jack said as he swung the car round to the base of the front steps.

Courtney's eyes narrowed on the slump in Agnes's shoulders and the curve in her back she hadn't noticed before. Jack was right. Agnes was older than she'd thought, and looking it.

Courtney's heart squeezed tight. Poor old thing. The death of her best friend had really knocked her for six; that and worrying about Crosswinds' debts. Courtney had told her the truth before she'd left to go to Sydney. No one else, however. Just Agnes.

It had been great to give good news this morning.

Courtney was out of the car in a flash and up the sandstone steps. 'Hi, there, Aggie!' she said, planting a peck on Agnes's gaunt cheek. No hug. Hugging had never been allowed around Crosswinds. 'You can stop worrying now. I'm back safe and sound.'

Agnes squared her shoulders, her faded eyes showing a mixture of reluctant fondness and annoyance. 'I gave up worrying about you almost twenty years ago, girlie. Now, why don't you have some decent manners for a change and introduce me to our guest?'

Courtney turned to find Jack right behind her, carrying her small duffel bag and his much larger suitcase. He was smiling a devilishly charming smile. Damn, but he was almost irresistible when he smiled like that!

'If we waited for Courtney to find her manners,' he said teasingly, 'we'd be here all night. I'm Jack Falconer, investment broker to the rescue.' He dropped the cases at his feet and stretched out his right hand. 'And you must be Agnes, the heart and backbone of Crosswinds. Courtney has told me so many wonderful things about you.'

Agnes beamed whilst Courtney rolled her eyes.

'Well, isn't it nice to meet a true gentleman for once?' Agnes said. 'But, my, you're a big fellow, aren't you? I think we'll have to put you in the front room with the four-poster.'

Courtney opened her mouth to protest, because that big old bed had been the focus of her wilder sexual fantasies over the past few years and she didn't want to push her luck. It was going to be hard enough resisting Jack without thinking of him lying naked and spread-eagled on top of that burgundy velvet bedspread, feet and hands bound to those four perfectly positioned bedposts.

But she could hardly say that, could she? And she couldn't think of any other reason why Agnes shouldn't put Jack in that particular guest room.

When her mouth snapped shut again, Jack gave her a small, strangely triumphant smile, as though he knew what was going on in her head.

To add insult to injury, Biggs chose that moment to wake and jump down from the swing seat he'd been snoozing in, sauntering over to sniff Jack's hand, totally ignoring Courtney. Jack gave him a scratch behind the ears, whereby the traitorous animal practically drooled.

'Nice dog,' Jack said.

'Getting old now,' Agnes said. 'Like we all are.'

'Not you, Agnes. You're just a spring chicken.'

It was a corny line but Agnes loved it, brightening up no end. 'I've a good twenty years in me yet, young man,' she told him.

'What's that delicious smell?' Jack asked, sniffing the air. Biggs sniffed with him.

'I'm cooking a leg of pork. I hope you like baked dinners.'

Jack groaned the groan of a true baked-dinner devotee. '*Do* I like baked dinners? I'd kill for one, but I haven't found anyone who could cook them like my mother. My darling mum's been passed away for a good few years now. But if my memory serves me correctly, her baked pork dinner smelt just like that. What's the secret, Agnes?'

'It's the sage and onion you cook with it,' Agnes revealed smugly. 'Some people like apple with their pork, but apple's not a patch on sage and onion.'

'I couldn't agree more. I can't wait to eat it.'

'Dinner's at six on the dot. But you must be thirsty from your trip. Would you fancy a nice glass of sherry? I always have one around this time of day.'

Jack grinned at her. 'Agnes, you wicked corrupter,

you! Just let me drop these bags in the right rooms and I'll join you in that sherry.'

'Courtney, you take Jack upstairs and show him where everything is. Oh, and get him some fresh towels out of the linen press. Those big blue bathsheets Hilary bought last Christmas would be best. Jack's going to need something large, by the look of him. I'll go check the dinner and we'll meet up in the front living room in ten minutes or so.'

'Great,' Jack agreed.

Agnes bustled off, leaving Jack to face Courtney's droll expression. 'I know who's the wicked corrupter around here,' she said drily.

'And I'm glad to see your guard dog is on such good form,' Jack countered, still stroking Biggs behind the ears. When the dog suddenly dropped down and rolled over onto his back, offering his stomach to be rubbed, Jack obliged.

Courtney scowled at her pet, but Biggs was too deep in doggie heaven to notice, or care.

'Oh, for pity's sake,' she snapped, sweeping the cases up from where Jack had dropped them. 'Do stop spoiling that infernal dog and come along.'

CHAPTER NINE

BIGGS trotted into the house with them, slavishly staying by Jack's side and looking up at him with doleful eyes as they mounted the stairs. Jack resumed petting him behind the ears.

'You're not doing him any favours, you know,' Courtney remarked tartly as they reached the top landing. 'He'll start howling when Agnes puts him out tonight.'

'I thought you said he slept on your bed.'

'I lied.'

His blue eyes gleamed. 'You're afraid of me.'

Courtney glared at him. 'Too right I am. You know I fancy you and, being a typical male, you're not above using that fact to your advantage.'

'Like Larry did?'

'No, not like Larry did,' she snapped. 'For your information, I propositioned Larry, not the other way around.'

'That's pretty daring behaviour, for a virgin.'

Her chin lifted. 'I'm a pretty daring sort of girl.'

'I know. I'm depending on it.'

'See? You're doing it already. What's next? Are you going to dare me into going to bed with you? Or will you grab me and kiss me once we're alone, thinking I'll melt. Well, I won't melt, buster,' she warned. 'I'll knee you in your pride and joy so hard you won't be any good to any woman for quite some time.'

He grimaced. 'I'll keep that in mind if I ever feel like grabbing you and kissing you.'

'Do that!' She stalked off along the upstairs hallway,

dropping her bag by her door before carrying his case into the front room and dumping it at the foot of the dreaded bed. One glance at the velvet spread had her swivelling round to leave straight away. Unfortunately, Jack was at that moment sauntering through the door, his devoted dog-slave at his heels.

'Now, that's some bed,' he said as he walked towards her.

Courtney stiffened and backed into one of the bed-posts, her hands flying up ready to fight him off. 'Don't start, Jack,' she warned.

'I won't. I just wanted you to know that my offer's still open, in case you change your mind later tonight.' He stopped at a short arm's distance, reaching out to pick up a stray curl and loop it behind her ear. The feel of his fingers brushing against her ear broke the surface of her skin out in goose-bumps.

'I won't use any dirty tactics,' he went on, his eyes never leaving hers. 'Or pressure. Or passes. Though I suspect if I did you just *might* melt, and you know it. But that's not what I want from you.'

'And what is it that you want from me, Jack?' she asked, her voice strange. It wasn't like her to sound like that, all soft and husky.

'Everything,' he returned, and there was nothing soft in *his* voice. It was hard and determined and oh, so sexy.

The temptation was acute. To say *Yes, yes, you can have everything. Do* everything. It's what I want, what I need, what I crave.

Suddenly, it wasn't Jack tied naked to that bed in her mind but herself, helpless and mindless, writhing under his mouth, his hands, his body, moaning and groaning, crying out, begging.

The begging bit saved her.

God, the very thought of it. *Begging* some man. Begging *Jack*. No, no, no, that was not on!

'I'll just get you those towels,' she said, pleased to hear her voice had returned to normal. 'And, Biggs, you get yourself back downstairs. If Agnes catches you up here in the bedrooms, you'll be exiled to the stables.'

Biggs, who was terrified of the stable moggie, did a bolt for the stairs.

'And you,' she added, swinging back to Jack. 'You can get your mind back on the reason you came here.'

Jack smiled. 'If you insist.'

'I insist. Now…that brand spanking new door over there leads into your *en suite*, a recent addition for privileged and usually married guests. I'll be back with the towels in less than a jiffy, then we'd best get downstairs too. I don't want Agnes thinking things.'

'Would she?'

'There's nothing Agnes doesn't think me capable of, Jack. Having a quickie with a handsome hunk like you would probably come low on her list of my many sins.'

'Then why worry?'

'Because I care what the old dear thinks of me, especially now, with Mum gone and her future in my hands.'

Jack frowned. 'Ah, yes. Agnes's future…'

'If I ever had to sell Crosswinds, it would kill Agnes.'

'And you, Courtney? Would it kill you?'

'Probably. But not before I killed every single person who made it happen!'

'That was simply wonderful, Agnes,' Jack complimented as he sipped the last of his after-dinner cup of tea. 'I haven't had a meal like that in years.'

You'd be right there, Courtney thought tartly. Not too many fancy Sydney restaurants serve up baked pork and crackling, with pavlova for afters. And I can't imagine darling Katrina specialised in home cooking. Her talents would have lain elsewhere, with the emphasis on *lain*.

Irritated by her sarcastic thoughts, Courtney stood up abruptly, scraping back her chair on the polished wooden floor. 'If you'll excuse me, I have to go see if any foals are due tonight. No, don't get up, Jack. You stay here. It's pitch-black and pretty cold outside. Far better you tour the place with the benefit of daylight and sunshine. I shouldn't be too long. But, if I am, don't worry. Foals don't always do as they're told.'

'Fine.' Jack shrugged those broad shoulders of his. 'I'll give Agnes a hand while you're gone, loading up the dishwasher.'

'We don't have a dishwasher,' Agnes informed him.

The surprised look on Jack's face annoyed Courtney.

Actually, everything about Jack tonight was annoying her. His charm. His kindness to Agnes. But most of all the way he could make *her* feel, without any effort on his part. He only had to be in the same room now, to set her heart pounding and her mind racing in erotic directions.

The dining room at Crosswinds was not a small room, the table large by any standards. Eight high-backed chairs could easily be accommodated around it. And there was still room for a selection of corner cabinets and side-boards.

Courtney had dashed in and set the table earlier whilst Jack had been busy drinking sherry with Agnes in the front living room. She'd placed Jack down the end near the fireplace, herself right at the other end not far from the door. She'd even strategically positioned a bowl of flowers, the blooms big enough to block any direct view of the ever increasingly attractive Jack.

But it had been a futile gesture. Jack had simply whipped the vase away on entering, dumping it on a sideboard with the witty aside, 'Roses are red, violets are blue, but I'd really much rather look at you.'

And look at her he had. Curiously. Speculatingly. Seductively.

Physical passes weren't the only way to seduce a woman, she was beginning to realise. The right man could do it with words, or his eyes, or simply by being under the same roof.

Courtney decided then and there that she would stay down at the brood-mare barn for a good few hours, whether a mare was foaling or not.

'Agnes likes to wash her own dishes,' she told Jack coolly, 'but I'm sure you could help by drying up. Now, if I *am* held up, there's always the TV for entertainment. We have satellite. And there are plenty of books to read.' The shelves in the living room had an eclectic mix, from biographies to novels of all genres, as well as books on everything to do with horses and horse breeding.

'Don't worry about me,' Jack replied with annoying nonchalance. 'I'll be fine. Agnes and I are going to play Scrabble. Naturally, you're welcome to join us, if and when you return.'

'Courtney doesn't like games,' Agnes said.

'Really? Why not?'

'Too much luck involved,' Courtney said sharply.

'Actually, luck only plays a small part in most games,' Jack countered. 'Winning depends more on concentration and skill.'

'You're skilled at Scrabble, then?' she asked archly.

'Never played it before in my life.'

Agnes chuckled as she rose and started clearing the

table. 'Let's get this done in a hurry, then, young man. After which you can come into my parlour…'

Jack stood up, laughing, his teeth flashing white. Courtney groaned silently and fled the room.

As it turned out, a mare *was* foaling when she arrived at the brood-mare barn, so she stayed and helped the night manager deliver the stylish bay colt. It was good to put her mind to something else for a couple of hours, other than that infernal man.

The birth was slow, and a bit tricky, and she was covered in blood by the time the new arrival slipped out into the waiting bed of straw.

'Glad that's over,' Fred said with a relieved sigh. 'I hate it when their legs get all tangled up like that. The mare panics. It was great to have an extra pair of hands to keep her calm. You're damned good at that, Courtney. You have just the right touch.'

The right touch…

The longing was back straight away, and so was the need, so sharp she almost cried out. In sheer desperation she stared at Fred. He wasn't a bad-looking man. Not the brightest, but still male. He wouldn't knock her back. Maybe if she…

Bile rose from her stomach to sting her throat. She gulped it down, even more panicky now. Because now she knew, knew that the thought of touching any man other than Jack revolted her so much that it made her sick.

Oh, God…

'Something wrong?' Fred asked.

Courtney shook her head. 'Just wool-gathering. You be all right by yourself for the rest of the night?'

'Sure. Nothing else doing here tonight. Next week things'll begin to hot up a bit, though. Then you might be losing some sleep. You'd better get back up to the house and to bed while you got the chance, I reckon.'

Courtney wished he hadn't said that.

'I think I'll go for a walk first,' she said. 'I like looking at the horses in the moonlight.'

It was chiming midnight on the grandfather clock in the hall by the time she tiptoed up the stairs. A light still glowed under the door of Jack's bedroom, which didn't exactly help her state of mind. Wretched man! Why couldn't he have been sound asleep, with everything in darkness? Why did she now have to contend with the thought of him lying there, still wide awake, his beautiful body ready and willing?

Gritting her teeth, she crept into her own room opposite his, snatching up a nightie from underneath her pillow and creeping back down the hallway to the far bathroom, hoping against hope that Jack wouldn't hear the shower running. She was careful in closing the old wooden door, then turning the big brass key in the lock.

Washing herself under the shower proved a torment. Her breasts felt full, her nipples electrified, and the area between her legs on fire. She tried to be quick, and not linger over sensitive spots, but the second she slid the soap over her private parts, she groaned. The temptation to keep doing it was acute. All she had to do was close her eyes and think about Jack, and surely...

'Damn it all, no!' she muttered. 'This is not what I want.'

She wanted Jack. Only Jack.

The soap clattered to the floor and her hand shot up to snap off the shower. She didn't bother with her nightie. A towel would do, wrapped tightly around her wet, heat-drenched body. Her hair hung in damp curls around her bared shoulders but she didn't give a fig about her hair.

She was past the point of no return, past caring about anything but finding some peace for her poor, pathetic, frustrated flesh.

How she had the forethought to return to her room for the box of condoms surprised her. At least she wasn't that far gone that she couldn't think of protection.

Her hesitation over the knob on Jack's door irritated the death out of her. Having made her decision, any lack of courage at this stage was not to be tolerated. It was just that he'd be so annoyingly smug and triumphant!

Too late to worry about that, she resolved boldly.

Opening the door, she slipped inside his room.

CHAPTER TEN

HE WAS asleep. Sound asleep. Sprawled out on the bed, one of the lamps still on, a book lying open on the pillow beside him. The remnants of a fire smouldered in the marble fireplace, making the room quite warm, which was possibly why he'd thrown back the sheets and was lying there wearing nothing but a pair of navy blue satin boxer shorts with some kind of jazzy red design all over them.

Feeling even more frustrated, Courtney stalked over and glared down at it.

Hearts, they were. Red hearts. Not the sort of thing a man would buy himself. Probably a Valentine's day present from a woman. No…from Superbitch.

Courtney practically ground her teeth. Did he think of her every time he put them on? Did he like sleeping in them, remembering how good she'd been in bed? Or how deliciously bad?

Piqued by her thoughts and by the fact that Jack hadn't tossed and turned into the night with wanting *her*, Courtney snatched up the book, snapped it shut and glared at the title.

'*How To Breed Champions*,' she read aloud, then glared at *him*. 'Breeding champions is not your job, buster,' she muttered, tossing the book onto a nearby dresser. 'Your job is to stay awake long enough for me to change my mind and take you up on your offer.'

'Your wish is my command…' His eyes flicked open as he rolled over and looked up at her through long dark lashes. 'Mmm. Glad to see you didn't overdress for the occasion.' And, reaching out, he tugged at the bottom of her towel.

It dropped to the floor, leaving her stark naked before him, clutching a box of condoms.

'You were awake all the time!' she accused.

'Not quite. But I certainly am now.' His hooded gaze travelled slowly over her from head to toe, drinking in every inch of her stiffly held nudity.

Do something, she ordered herself. Don't just stand there like some undressed dummy in a shop window.

'You are one beautiful woman, Courtney Cross,' he said thickly. 'Now, come here...'

It was a softly voiced order. A seductive order.

How easy it would have been to fall into his arms and let him do as he willed.

It was a struggle to find the boldly assertive creature she usually became when she wanted sex. Because it wasn't just sex she was secretly craving this time, was it? It was the mindless ecstasy of total surrender.

Which made it all the more imperative that she follow her usual path.

'Now, Jack,' she said firmly, and busied herself ripping the Cellophane off the box of condoms. 'I told you. I like to be at the wheel. Besides, you must be tired after all that driving today. That's why you fell asleep with the light on. So just lie back, relax and let *me* take responsibility for everything. You'll enjoy it. Trust me.'

The Cellophane gone, she flipped open the box and tossed it onto the bedside table before pushing Jack onto his back and climbing up onto the bed beside him.

He looked taken aback when she immediately started pulling down his boxer shorts. 'Hey! What the heck do...?'

Too late. His shorts were already off.

'Do be quiet, Jack. Agnes is not a heavy sleeper. We don't want her coming in to find out what all the noise is about, do we?'

His dark brows lifted but he eventually lay back and shut his mouth. Which was good, Courtney told herself. She didn't like her men to talk. She wasn't there for a tête-à-tête. She was there to soothe her galloping hormones, or whatever it was Jack had evoked in her to such a maddeningly compulsive level.

'Now,' she murmured, straddling his wonderfully muscular thighs then sitting back on his knees. 'Let's have a look at you...'

If she'd been struggling for control before, now was the real moment of truth, with Jack naked and immobile beneath her, his magnificently macho body on full display for her hungry gaze.

And hungry she was. Oh, so hungry. As her eyes raked over him she wanted to ravish him on the spot. Every single bit of him.

Courtney tried telling herself his body was no better than any she'd seen before. Just bigger. And bigger wasn't necessarily better.

Or so some stupid fool had told her once. Some people simply had no idea.

'You are one beautiful man, Jack Falconer,' she murmured, and leant forward to run her hands all over his wonderfully hairy chest, his smooth-as-satin shoulders, his strong upper arms. Her breathing became ragged as she moved back to his chest again, where her fingers splayed sensuously within the mass of soft dark curls.

He gasped when they grazed over his nipples.

When his hands reached for *her*, she grabbed his wrists and pushed them into the pillows on either side of his head, a position that unfortunately had the tips of her breasts brushing against the hair of his chest. For a second or two, she almost lost it.

His smiling at her snapped her back to the potential disaster of this situation.

'I'm the driver tonight, remember?' she whispered harshly against his lips. 'Not you. No touching,' she commanded. 'No moving. No nothing. Do you think you can manage that for once?'

'Yes, boss,' he replied, but he was still smiling.

She kissed him, deep and hard, a powerful punishing kiss which was supposed to tell him who, indeed, was boss. But once again it was herself in danger of losing control. If he'd been able to put his hands on her, she might have. As it was, she kept her head. Just.

As for Jack, he was breathing very heavily by the time she wrenched her mouth away from his and straightened up again. His eyes had darkened to slate and he was no longer smiling. His erection spoke for itself, lying huge and high against his stomach.

'You sure you know what you're doing, here?' Jack muttered thickly when she reached to encircle it with both her hands.

She sucked in a steadying breath, swallowed, then gave him what she hoped was a cool smile.

Her hands began to move and his eyes widened, his body flinching each time her thumb grazed over the soft velvety tip. Finally, his hips began to lift slightly from the bed, his buttocks squeezing tightly together.

'You'd better stop doing that,' he growled.

Courtney stopped, squeezing him in exactly the right spot so that he immediately subsided. Jack looked stunned whilst she tried to hide her own rattled state. She hadn't meant to let things go quite that far with just her

hands, but she'd become mesmerised by his responses to
her touch, by his actually becoming longer and thicker
and harder. She'd thought he was fully erect.

'Courtney, *no*.' Jack groaned when she bent her mouth
to where her hands had been. 'For pity's sake!'

But pity was not an emotion Courtney was feeling at
that moment. Her whole being was consumed by the most
compelling need to possess him again. Utterly. And far
more intimately. There was no cohesive thought on her
part. Just the sense of herself falling into a black abyss
from which there was no escape.

Her heart lurched as her lips closed over him, her head
swirled and, finally, she was lost to the darkness.

His abrupt pulling her off him and up to his mouth
came as a shock, much like someone suddenly shining a
blinding light into your sleepy eyes.

'Time to change driver, honey,' he grated out.

Dazed and disorientated, Courtney was like a rag doll
as he rolled her over onto her back, his mouth crushing
down onto hers. This time it was *his* tongue darting deep,
his hands holding her arms out wide and *his* body pressing her down, down, down.

Panic had her struggling to break free, her mouth twist-
ing from his with a harsh cry of protest.

'Hush up,' he ground out. 'You can be on top another
night, but right now you're going to be made love to by
a real man for a change, not some bloody puppet you
can pull around by the strings. My name's not Larry,
honey. It's Jack. And, like I said, I don't take orders.
Now, are you going to be co-operative and quiet? Or do
I have to kiss you till you are?'

Her eyes were like saucers, but her mouth stayed silent.

'Good.'

He still kissed her, over and over, kissed her till she was reeling, and then…then he started kissing her all over. Her throat. Her breasts. Her stomach. Her thighs. Between her thighs.

'Oh, God,' she moaned, and spread her legs wider for him.

This was one of the things she'd feared; what she'd worried might happen to her. That she would be powerless to stop him doing whatever he liked. And here it was, happening to her.

Yet the reality wasn't anything to fear, she eventually realised. It was…bliss.

'Don't stop,' she choked out when he did.

His laughter was dark. 'Can't have you getting too addicted to that. Or coming too soon.'

She groaned. She'd been awfully close.

He kissed his way back up her body till he got to her breasts again. There, he sucked on her nipples till they were so sensitive just breathing on them made her tremble and arch her back.

By the time he reached for the condom she was quivering, and panting. She could not wait for the moment when she could feel him entering her, filling her totally. She bent her knees in readiness, breathless with anticipation.

'You like it like that?' he asked, sounding surprised. 'In the missionary position?'

She blinked, startled that he was stopping to discuss positions at this stage when she was just dying to have him inside her, any old way.

'Sometimes,' she lied, and he shrugged.

'Not many women do. But that's okay. I'm easy.'

She gasped as he entered her, his thick, hard length thrusting home in one solid surge. Her legs automatically lifted to wrap themselves tight around him, as did her arms, winding around his big broad back, holding him close, pulling him even deeper into her.

The sensation was incredible. 'Oh, Jack...'

'I know,' he muttered. 'I know. I feel it too.'

Did he? she wondered dazedly. Did he really?

She'd never known anything like it. Not just the physical pleasure, but something else. A wave crashing through her, a wave of emotion so strong it took everything with it, especially all her preconceptions and misconceptions about making love with Jack.

Her heart filled with it, overflowed with it. She hugged him to her and wanted nothing but to stay that way forever, their flesh fused, their hearts beating as one.

This had to be love, she realised in her rapture, that long-scorned emotion that she scarcely believed in and told herself she would never fall victim too.

Love. Glorious, wonderful, overwhelming love.

Jack began to move, making her gasp and forcing her mind back to the physical reality of the moment, which was Jack, thrusting powerfully into her, Jack, having sex with her.

It wasn't love for him, was it?

Everything inside her contracted, with emotional pain not sexual pleasure. Yet it possibly felt the same to him, for he moaned and stopped momentarily. She stared up at him with hopeless longing, and he stared back down at her, an odd expression crossing his already strained face.

And then he did something that threw Courtney into total despair. He closed his eyes, and sighed.

He's thinking of her, she agonised. Maybe even pretending I'm her. That's what that weird look was all about. And that sigh.

Immediately, she wanted him gone from her. Away. Out of her body!

But no sooner had that angry thought swept through her than he began to move again, and she gasped, stunned at the pleasure he could still bring, even when she knew what she was to him. A cypher. A stand-in. A second-rate substitute.

Suddenly she understood her mother's bitterness towards her father. She must have fallen in love with him too. But he hadn't loved her back. That was his crime, not loving her back, whilst still being able to enjoy her body and forcing her to enjoy his.

Courtney tried not to enjoy Jack's body. Tried to switch off. But it was too late. Either that or she was too weak. Loving Jack was making her weak. Terribly weak.

Finally, she didn't even try to fight her feelings. Impossible, anyway. They were consuming her with a heat and a passion so strong that nothing short of a bomb falling on this bed was going to stop her seeing this out to its inevitable end.

Her first spasm had her sucking air sharply into her lungs. She might have screamed out, but his mouth crashed down on hers again, muffling her cries into soft moans, making her head spin even as the spasms went on and on and on. His big arms wrapped round her and he scooped her up from the bed, clutching her hard to him as he came too, shuddering and shaking. He buried his head in her hair, muttering things she couldn't quite make out.

Finally the tempest was over, and an awkward stillness descended on both of them. An awkward silence as well.

Jack's rather weary sigh spelled things out for Courtney.

Hard to keep pretending once the heat of the moment

was over and cold reality returned. Reality being a simple country girl with long dark hair, not a glamorous city-smart blonde who no doubt didn't fancy the missionary position at all, but all sorts of other exotic and erotic ways.

Courtney had used to think she knew it all when it came to seducing men. Yet what did she really know, other than being on top along with some elementary oral techniques? Hardly the stuff sex goddesses were made of.

Courtney's despair deepened. *Jack is never going to fall in love with me, not after Katrina. All I can hope for is a superficial friendship, sex every night he's here, and maybe the odd one-night stand whenever I come to Sydney.*

An hour ago Courtney could have coped with that quite well.

Now it would hurt her more than she could ever have envisaged. Yet, at the same time, she knew she wouldn't say no. She'd be there, at his beck and call, for as long as he wanted her.

That was the truth of it. Better to accept the harsh reality of a one-sided love, otherwise she might end up as bitter and twisted as her mother.

Besides, Jack was not a bad man. Just the opposite. He was a very nice man. He wasn't out to deliberately hurt her, or to callously use her. He thought she was on his wavelength, wanting nothing more from their relationship than what he'd offered right from the start.

An affair.

Now it was up to her to keep that status quo, as well as her pride. There would be no dramatic confession of love. No desperate tactics to try to get him to fall in love with her. Hell, no. She wasn't playing sweet little thing for any man. Or *femme fatale*, either. She was what she was and he could take her or leave her.

Which meant he would probably do both.

It would hurt, but she'd survive. Of course she would. She'd been brought up tough.

But first, how to extricate herself from Jack's arms without his twigging to anything being wrong?

Their position was still highly intimate and extrication potentially embarrassing. Jack was sitting on his haunches in the middle of the bed with her clasped tightly against his torso, her buttocks resting on his thighs, their bodies still intimately locked together.

'Er…um…Jack…?'

'Mmm?' His head remained buried in her hair.

'I…I need to go to bed. I have to be up early.'

He groaned, and lifted his head, his blue eyes soft and dreamy. 'I don't want you to go,' he murmured. 'I want you to stay with me.'

'I can't,' she replied, trying not to show alarm. Because she wanted to, oh, so much, wanted to wallow in his arms and in his lovemaking, if not for the rest of her life, then at least for one whole night.

But Agnes was an early riser and she simply didn't dare.

'I don't know about you, but I'm exhausted,' she went on, using every ounce of her will-power to sound cool and calm. 'We can spend more time together tomorrow night.'

His smile was wry. 'Can I trust you not to change your mind again?'

Oh, God. Little did he know.

'After that magnificent performance?'

'Same time tomorrow night, then?' he suggested.

'A little earlier perhaps.' She knew she wouldn't be

able to wait till midnight a second time. 'I never could resist a bargain.'

Surprisingly, he didn't laugh at her joke. Instead, he frowned. 'What about Agnes?'

'Agnes is usually in bed by ten-thirty.'

'What kept *you* so long tonight?'

Fear of coming back and falling in love with you.

'A foal. A gorgeous little colt.' Her face softened at the thought of it, valiantly struggling to its feet so soon after birth. 'A darling thing. But he gave the mare a bit of a hard time. I had to sit there in the straw for ages, stroking her neck and telling her it was going to be all right.'

'Which it was?'

'Oh, yes. Mother and baby doing fine.'

He gave her an odd look, as though he wanted to say something but wasn't sure if it was a good idea. 'Courtney…'

'Yes?'

'Just now, when we were making love…' His hesitation brought a tightening to her heart.

'Yes?' she asked warily. *Don't you dare tell me that,* her eyes informed him. *I don't need to know. That would be cruel.*

He sighed again. Damn, but she hated those sighs. 'Nothing. It was fantastic. That's all. *You're* fantastic. I just wanted you to know that.'

She smiled through her heartbreak. 'Thanks, lover. But you're the one who was fantastic. I can't wait till tomorrow night.' And wasn't that the truth? 'Meanwhile, don't forget your promise to be discreet. No giveaways, please, when other people are around. No sneaky little kisses or hand-holding, or any of that mushy stuff. I mean…we don't have to do that, do we? We both know the score here. It's not as though we're besotted lovers. We're adults, enjoying a nice little discreet fling. Isn't that right?'

Deny it, she willed wildly as she looked up at him. *Tell me it isn't so. Tell me you're madly besotted with me, that you can't keep your hands off me, that you want me by your side till we die!*

The feverish desperation of her thoughts disgusted her, and she looked away. Love had turned her into a fool. A stupid, romantic, female fool.

Oh, Mum. I know what you suffered now.

But she hated the thought of becoming bitter like her mother. Somehow, she had to stop that happening.

'I really must go now, Jack,' Courtney said truthfully enough, calmer eyes swinging back up to his.

The most seductive passion glittered in his eyes.

'And I really don't want you to go.'

'That's very flattering, but I really think that—'

His mouth obliterated the rest of her words.

Courtney was to be appalled later to realise it took him all of five seconds' flat to change her mind.

CHAPTER ELEVEN

COURTNEY rolled over, blinked blearily, and finally focused on her bedside clock.

'Good grief!' she exclaimed, and leapt from the bed. 'Ten-thirty!'

Seven minutes later she was showered, dressed and hurrying downstairs, her hands scooping her hair up into a ponytail on the way. She burst into the kitchen, startled to find Agnes, Jack and Sarah sitting at the kitchen table, sipping cups of tea.

The trio glanced up at her as she rushed through the door, both Jack and Sarah saying good morning and smiling whilst Agnes rose to move over to the stove. Sarah was especially effusive in her greeting, which was not like her at all.

A widow, Sarah Pearson had come to work at Crosswinds twenty years before, shortly after her gamblerholic husband had shot himself, leaving her with three teenage daughters to raise on her own. At the time of his suicide, Reg Pearson had been working at Crosswinds as a general handyman, and the stud had been a much smaller concern. Hilary had taken pity on the destitute Sarah and had created a job for her as secretary and office manager, even though Sarah hadn't been able to type back then.

Now fifty-seven, Sarah was still not the greatest typist in the world. Neither was she a great man-lover. Her bright smile, plus the colour in her plump cheeks this morning, made it apparent Jack had already been working his effortless charm on her.

The silly stab of jealousy this thought evoked made Courtney resolve to avoid Jack during daylight hours, confining her weakness for him to those private moments behind closed doors. She would not be able to function properly as the boss of Crosswinds if she kept thinking about him and the ease with which he had seduced her to his will last night.

She hadn't returned to her own bed till after three. No wonder she'd slept like the dead.

But what of the man himself? He had to be some kind of machine to do what he'd done and pop back up this morning looking perkier than a buck-rabbit in springtime.

There he sat, sipping tea and smiling up at her over the rim of his cup, looked totally refreshed and relaxed. Yet it was clear he'd been up for some time, if the empty breakfast plates beside him were any guide. He was wearing the stone-washed jeans he'd worn the previous day, but with a different top, a blue Sloppy Joe which made his eyes look bluer than the bluest outback sky.

'Someone should have woken me up,' she said to no one in particular as she set about making herself a mug of instant coffee.

'Jack thought you deserved a sleep in,' Sarah said.

Courtney finished making the black sugarless coffee before slowly turning, a cool smile hiding her pounding heart.

'Really?' Her eyes met his directly.

His eyebrows lifted ever so slightly in what she saw as a wickedly knowing gesture, and suddenly she was back in his bed, boneless after another mind-blowing orgasm, begging him to stop, then begging him not to.

Truly, she'd never known such orgasms existed. What

she'd been experiencing all these years paled by comparison.

Being in love with your lover certainly made a difference. As did the skill of that lover. Jack was everything Courtney had dreamt, yet feared he'd be. Demanding, yet giving. Dominating, yet not selfish. A sensualist of the first order, infinitely tender and gently coercing. It had been so easy to close her eyes and pretend that he loved her. No man could have been more loving in his lovemaking. That was the most seductive part of all.

But he didn't love her. She really couldn't afford to forget that, or Lord knew what other stupidities she might fall victim to. Being his love slave every night of his stay was going to be bad enough!

'You had a very long weekend,' he said, his eyes never leaving hers. 'The trip down to Sydney on Friday, the races on Saturday, driving back on Sunday. Then a late night last night on top of that. You had to have been exhausted.'

Courtney decided she wasn't going to indulge in word games or *double entendres*. Jack might like that kind of thing, but she didn't.

'Yes, I was very tired,' she said. 'You're right. But now it's Monday morning and time to get back to business. Have you had the opportunity yet to ask Sarah about all those things you wanted to know?' Presumably, by now, Sarah had been informed of the lie of the land.

'We've only just touched the surface, haven't we, Sarah?'

'Oh, yes. Barely. It's going to take most of the day, if Jack wants a detailed history of every horse you own. At last count, Crosswinds had over sixty brood mares. And then there's the three stallions, the yearlings and all those horses Hilary leased out for racing.'

'No worries,' Courtney said. 'I'm going to be busy all day myself, doing the rounds with Ned. It's busy, busy, busy at this time of year, isn't it, Agnes?'

Agnes glanced around from where she was cooking Courtney her usual breakfast of scrambled eggs on toast. 'It certainly is. And, speaking of Ned, he was here looking for you a little while ago. I said you'd go see him as soon as you'd had breakfast. He said to tell you he'd be at the breeding barn.'

'Right.' Courtney started sipping her mug of steaming coffee. 'Did he say what he wanted me for?' she asked, and a tiny icicle of apprehension trickled down her spine.

'No. But he didn't look all that happy.'

'I wonder what he's doing down at the breeding barn? I mean…the season hasn't started yet.'

'Maybe the roof has sprung a leak,' Sarah piped up. 'It's pretty old, you know. Most of the buildings have leaky roofs, the office included.'

'Yes, I know,' Courtney said grimly, her mind well and truly back on the problems at Crosswinds. She'd forgotten them for a while, there. 'Let's hope we can do something about that soon,' she added, and turned a matter-of-fact face Jack's way. 'How long do you think it will take to get the money, if your investor decides he's in?'

'Barely any time at all. He might have to sell a few stocks and shares, but that only takes minutes.'

'In that case, how long do you think before you'll be able to give him the go-ahead? And before you say it, yes, I know you'll want to be satisfied Crosswinds is a going concern with potential for future profits first. I'm assuming you'll be happy with what Sarah shows you. And what you see here in general. As I said before, shabby fences and leaky buildings mean nothing. They are not the value in a stud. It's the land itself, plus the brood mares and stallions. And ours are second to none.'

'I appreciate that. Look, it shouldn't take me too long. After Sarah's input today, I'll need to speak to your accountant. Perhaps you could arrange an appointment for tomorrow? Then I'd like to spend the rest of the week just getting the feel of the place, seeing how things run on a more personal level. I often rely on my gut instinct, not just facts and figures, when it comes to an investment. I'd say by next weekend I should be satisfied, one way or another.'

Courtney frowned and wondered if she was reading between the lines correctly here. What did he really mean by 'the feel of the place', and 'on a more personal level'? Exactly what kind of satisfaction was he referring to? Was he implying that if she kept him happy in bed all week he'd recommend the investment?

Shock at this last thought held her speechless for a split second. She hadn't expected such scurrilous behaviour from a man who'd nobly paid off debts he hadn't personally incurred. But she supposed men could never be trusted when it came to matters of sex and ego.

As for herself... She was a goner anyway when it came to resisting him sexually. So she might as well use that to secure her investor. But it put a nasty taste in her mouth. Hopefully, she was wrong about this. But if she wasn't?

Courtney smothered a sigh. Who did she think she was kidding? She would still do whatever was necessary to save Crosswinds.

A knock on the back door interrupted her troubled thoughts.

It was Ned, looking more than a little worried.

Although only forty-four, Ned's outdoor lifestyle in the

Australian sun, plus his hatred of hats, had left him with a very lined face. But some of the lines at that moment were clearly coming from stress. Or *dis*tress.

Serious alarm bells started ringing in Courtney's head. Ned was not a man easily rattled, or upset. He had a laid-back, laconic style which suited the handling of highly strung horses.

'What is it, Ned?'

'We have a serious problem with one of the stallions, boss.'

Courtney liked it that he called her boss, the same as he'd called her mother. Not that she expected it from anyone else around Crosswinds. Most just called her Courtney.

'Which one?'

'Goldplated.'

Oh, no...

'He's not sick, is he?' she asked, feeling sick herself at such a prospect.

'Nope. Nothing like that.'

'What is it, then?'

'Best come and see for yourself.'

She heard a chair scrape back on the wooden floor behind her.

'I'll come with you,' Jack said, materialising by her side.

'Very well,' Courtney bit out. She could hardly refuse. There was also no point in keeping the reason for Jack's presence here a secret any longer, though Ned needn't know the *full* extent of her debt. 'This is Jack Falconer, Ned. He's a financial expert, up here from Sydney to look over Crosswinds with a view to finding me a business partner. You know how strapped for cash we are around here. So get used to seeing him around this week. Jack, this is Ned Meggitt, my stud foreman.'

'Pleased to meet you, Ned,' Jack said, holding out his hand.

Ned looked impressed with Jack's handshake.

'Same here,' he replied. 'Know anything about horses?'

'They kick one end and bite the other?'

Ned glanced at Courtney. 'He doesn't look like a city-slicker, but he sure sounds like one. Which is perhaps just as well…'

With this last cryptic remark, Ned turned away abruptly to start walking down the back path which led past the rose garden and down towards the stud proper.

'After you,' Jack said, waving Courtney ahead of him through the wire-screen door.

'Looks like breakfast will have to wait, Agnes.' She dumped her coffee and snatched up the fawn Akubra which was hanging on a peg near the back door. Planting it firmly on her head, she set off after the rapidly disappearing Ned. Jack caught up quickly to stride out beside her.

'You look like a cowgirl in that hat,' he said, slanting her an admiring glance. 'A very sexy cowgirl.'

She ground to a brief but very necessary halt. 'Let's get one thing straight, Jack. Keep the flattery for the bedroom. It'll work very well there. Out here, however, I'm nothing to you but a business client. I told you this before. Have I made myself perfectly clear this time?'

'Crystal,' he bit out, not looking pleased at all. Which was just too bad. He couldn't have *everything* his way.

'Good,' she snapped, then marched on after Ned, leaving Jack in her wake.

It was quite some distance from the house to the breeding barn. The wide gravel path wound its way down between the large brood-mare yards on the left and grazing pastures on the right. Overhead, it was another sunny day, but not exactly warm at this hour in the morning. Nights in the valley were colder than in Sydney and the air on clear winter days always stayed crisp till after lunch.

Courtney didn't feel at all cold, however, as she hurried along. She was too preoccupied to feel anything as mundane as cold. Guilt was worming its way into her head and heart. Yet why *should* she feel guilty about putting Jack back into his place? He knew the score. Just now he'd been deliberately trying to cross the line she'd drawn for him. And she just wouldn't have it!

Being in love with him made it all the more crucial she not let him take advantage of that fact. Of course, he didn't *know* she was in love with him, but he knew she fancied him: fancied him so much that all he'd had to do last night was start kissing her again and all her will had dissolved.

Courtney groaned at the memory, and strode out all the faster, her head down, her thoughts in a whirl. She didn't realise Ned wasn't alone outside the breeding barn doors till she practically ran into the stranger standing next to him.

'Oh!' she gasped, stepping back, then staring at the man with startled eyes. He stared right back at her, his appraisal as curious and as thorough as the one she gave him.

He was of average height and an elegant build, with jet-black eyes, deeply tanned skin and close-cropped iron-grey hair. Though obviously middle-aged, he had the air of one much younger, possibly because he was dressed in tight black jeans and a black leather jacket. If he'd been less handsome, he might have looked stupid wearing such gear, like some aging biker who didn't know when to quit. As it was, he looked interesting and quite sexy, if you liked that type.

Courtney immediately thought of Lois. If these were her stables and this fellow was looking for a job, he'd be hired on the spot.

'And who are you?' she asked brusquely. 'Ned, you know we can't hire any more grooms at the moment.'

'The name's Sean, ma'am.' He had the most attractively lilting Irish accent. 'Sean O'Flannery.'

'Courtney Cross,' she returned as she took his hand and shook it.

'Yes, ma'am. I know who *you* are. And no, I haven't come here for a job. I wanted to see you.'

'*See* me?'

'He's got some information you're not going to like,' Ned said gruffly. 'About Goldplated.'

Courtney glanced over her shoulder to see where Jack had got to. He was leaning on the fence just behind her, watching and listening.

Her gaze swung back to her visitor. 'Not good news, I take it?' she said.

'Not the best.'

'Out with it, then.'

The man's eyes moved in Jack's direction. 'I don't think this is news you'll want spread around.'

'Don't worry about Jack. He'll have to know, sooner or later,' she added drily.

'Fine. Look, I'm really sorry to have to tell you this, but all the mares supposedly serviced by Goldplated at his first season were artificially inseminated. He didn't cover a single one. He refused to.'

Courtney went cold all over. My God, if this was true...

'How do you know this?' she demanded to know.

'I was working there at the time. I was Gold Fever's personal groom last season.'

'Goldplated's full brother?'

He nodded.

Courtney's mind whirled with all sorts of dreadful possibilities. 'They used *his* sperm instead of Goldplated's?'

'No. Goldplated's progeny are all genetically his, all right. But unless there's been a radical change in your new stallion's behaviour since last year, he won't willingly perform this year, either.'

'Oh, my God.'

'You can say that again,' Ned growled. 'When Sean told me all this, I couldn't believe it. So I thought I'd give the horse a trial run, so to speak. I got one of the stock mares who's in season and tied her up in the breeding barn. Then I went and got Goldplated out of his yard. He was like a lamb till I took him inside the barn. He got one sniff of the mare and just went berserk. I've never seen anything like it. Frightened the poor mare to death. Frightened *me* to death too. I was lucky to get her out of there before any damage was done. I left Goldplated in there till he calmed down and saw there wasn't anything to fear in the barn itself.'

Courtney could only shake her head in despair. No wonder her mother had bought the horse at that bargain price. Whatever was she going to do now? Crosswinds always provided a photo of the actual service with any outside booking, a guarantee for owners that they were getting what they paid for.

Jack tapped her on the shoulder. 'Can you sue the people who sold you the horse?' he asked.

'Maybe. But suing takes lots of money and time. And

it's always dicey, especially when the other party is so rich. The owners of Gold Fever are billionaires.'

'So why on earth would they do something as dishonest as this?'

'They didn't know,' Sean revealed. 'It was the stud master's doing. Plus his fault in the first place.'

Courtney frowned. 'What do you mean?'

'That's the right word. Mean. Mean and stupid. When Goldplated first arrived at stud he was still a very young horse, all hyped up from the track. The stud master didn't give him enough time to let down, and calm down. I gather Goldplated kicked him the first time they tried to get him to cover a mare. Probably more out of excitement than anything. It was just an accident. But the stupid fella lost his temper and lashed out with a whip.'

'You're joking!' Courtney was appalled.

'Unfortunately, no.' Sean looked totally disgusted as well. 'As if you can teach a young horse stud duties with a whip! It's no wonder the poor animal goes off his brain when he's brought near a mare in heat. He's probably expecting his handler to turn on him at any moment. If you look, you'll find two deep scars across his forehead. They're quite high, under his forelock.'

Courtney groaned. 'They said he'd done that rearing up in the starting gates.'

'Yeah, they would. But that's not the case. You've got yourself a fine young stallion in Goldplated, Ms Cross, but he's been badly mishandled. Personally, I believe he could still come good, but it'll take patience and some lateral thinking.'

'Why did you decide to tell me this?' she asked, puzzled. 'You didn't have to.'

'I felt badly when I heard your mother had been the one who bought Goldplated. She has a fine reputation in the horse world. I didn't like to think of her being cheated like that.'

Courtney looked at him thoughtfully. He'd taken his time coming to tell her, then. It had been months since her mother had bought the horse. Maybe he'd come because he *did* want a job.

'I gather you're no longer Gold Fever's groom?'

'No. I usually move on pretty regularly. I get bored staying in one place for long.'

'How good *are* you with stallions, Sean?'

His smile was wry. 'Damned good. Even if I say so myself.'

'Do you think you might be able to do something with Goldplated by exercising some of that patience and lateral thinking you spoke of?'

'I'd sure like to try.' His smile widened.

Darn, but he was a good-looking man for his age. Lois would go ape, if she ever saw him. Which she just might. She was due up soon.

'You're hired, then,' Courtney said, and smiled.

'But boss,' Ned protested, 'you just said we couldn't afford to hire any more staff.'

'One more isn't going to make much difference.' She wouldn't draw any salary herself for a while. She didn't need anything, anyway. Courtney turned to face Jack. 'Besides, if we don't get Goldplated serving mares the natural way this season, there might not be jobs for anyone at Crosswinds before long. Isn't that right, Jack?'

'I'm afraid so. I couldn't possibly advise anyone to invest here with a cloud hanging over Goldplated's ability to perform.'

Her chin rose. 'In that case, we'll just have to make sure he *does* perform. Sean, do you think you might be able to work a major miracle in less than a month?'

He didn't bat an eyelid. 'No sweat, Ms Cross. I already have a plan in mind.'

Courtney was surprised by his cool confidence, yet for some reason she had faith in the man. Maybe it was his eyes. He had clever eyes. 'That's wonderful,' she said, smiling up at him. 'And it's Courtney, please. Not Ms Cross or ma'am. We don't stand on ceremony here. Ned, show him up to the office and get Sarah to sign him on as a casual. Now, Sean, you have the option of bed and board here or perhaps finding a place in Queenswood. A lot of my staff are locals anyway, but some do live in.'

'I'll live in.'

'In that case I'll apologise in advance for the staff's quarters. They're in urgent need of a make over.'

'Well, I'm a dab hand with a paintbrush,' he offered. 'Fact is, I'm a bit of a jack of all trades. So don't hesitate to ask if you need anything else done around the place.'

'That's a very generous offer, Sean,' she said. 'I'll certainly keep it in mind, but your first priority is Goldplated. Perhaps we might have a chat later this afternoon over what you have in mind for him. Okay?'

'Fine by me.'

'See you later, then. Oh, and take Jack with you, Ned,' she added sharply. 'He has business with Sarah.'

'What about you?' Jack retorted.

'I have breakfast to eat, an accountant to ring up and a million and one other jobs to do. I'll see you tonight at dinner, Jack. Have a good day.'

Courtney turned her back on him and marched off. But not before she'd seen the stiffening in his jaw muscles, and the harsh resolve in his narrowed eyes.

Till tonight, honey, they seemed to say. *Then we'll see who's boss...*

CHAPTER TWELVE

IT WAS a long, long day.

Courtney skipped lunch, partly because she was avoiding Jack and partly because she didn't have much of an appetite. She wasn't sure if it was the problem with Goldplated causing her to feel so churned up, or the thought of the night ahead, with Jack.

Whatever, she went from job to job, frantic to keep busy. She did some trackwork on a horse they were trying to get fit after a long spell, the one Lois would be coming to pick up soon. She delivered and spread out fresh straw in the outdoor stables. She checked all the water troughs in the yards. She helped mix up feed. She also had a long and interesting chat with the new man, and thought his plan to cure Goldplated was so stunningly simple it just might work.

But even after that she felt no calmer inside, despite now having some real hope that Crosswinds might avert this new crisis.

So the problem had to be Jack.

Her problem was always going to be Jack from now on, wasn't it? Courtney conceded.

The sun had set by the time she gave in and returned to the house, the darkness of night rapidly descending as she kicked off her dusty boots at the veranda, then hung her equally dusty hat on the peg beside the front door.

A light was shining in the window of the main living room, which suggested that Jack and Agnes were already in there, sipping pre-dinner cream sherry and chatting away like old friends, a fact confirmed when Courtney popped her head in the door.

'I'm home,' she said.

'We were just going to send a search party out for you,' Jack said, looking relaxed in the big chintz armchair by the fire. Biggs was lying asleep at his feet, and didn't even raise an eyelid at his mistress's voice.

Miserable traitor, Courtney thought, before remembering Biggs was a boy dog. *Never trust a male,* her mother had always said. *They have no sense of loyalty. Their only priority in life is their own pleasure.*

And wasn't that the truth!

'Dinner is in fifteen minutes on the dot,' Agnes warned. 'But you don't have to set the table. Jack and I did it together.'

'Thanks,' she said, throwing Jack a sickly sweet smile. 'Won't be long. Just have to grab a shower and change.'

She trudged upstairs, muttering away to herself. Why it should bother her if Jack was nice to Agnes, she had no idea. It wasn't jealousy. Perhaps it was resentment that he might not be being sincere, that he was playing with Agnes, as he was playing with her. She hated the thought that this was all a game to him, whereas her feelings for him were dead serious. She loved the man to distraction.

As if to confirm just how much in love she was, she put her hair back in Lois's gold clip after her shower, and sprayed herself liberally with the perfumed deodorant she'd bought the previous day. She also donned not her usual jeans but a pair of figure-hugging black cut-offs and a soft V-necked black jumper which Lois had given her at the weekend.

'No more black clothes for me,' Lois had said. 'So you might as well have these too.'

Courtney had to admit she looked—and felt—quite

sexy in them, especially since she'd left off her bra. This wasn't as bold a move as it might have been if the jumper had been a lighter colour. Her nipples, despite feeling tight and tingly, weren't obvious at a glance. But her unfettered breasts moved like jelly as she hurried downstairs, making her intensely aware of her body, and how turned on she already was.

She loved—and loathed—the feeling. One part of her hated being powerless to control her passion for Jack, but the greater part of her wanted to wallow in it, to experience all there was to experience whilst he was here, to make memories which were probably going to have to last her a lifetime.

This last thought brought such a sharp pain to her heart that she stopped abruptly with a gasp, and clutched at the balustrade.

Jack chose just that moment to walk out of the room and catch her standing there, looking stricken. To give him credit, his eyes mirrored immediate concern. 'Are you all right?' he asked worriedly, and dashed around to leap up the stairs and put a gentle hand around her shoulder.

She just stared up at him. She'd heard of people dying of a broken heart. Was that going to be her fate when he left?

'What is it?' he demanded to know, eyes searching her strained face. 'Are you ill?'

'A…a pain,' she said truthfully. 'Like a vice. Here…' And she lifted a shaky hand from the balustrade to cover her heart.

He looked even more alarmed. 'You have some kind of heart trouble?'

'Not…not that I know of…' At least, not in any physical sense.

'Your mother died of a coronary, though, didn't she?'
She nodded.

'You should get yourself checked out, Courtney. Have an ultrasound. And an ECG. These things can sometimes be congenital.'

Agnes came out into the hallway. 'What is it? What's wrong?'

'Courtney had some kind of turn. It could be angina.'

Courtney swiftly pulled herself together at the shock on Agnes's face. She hadn't realised till that moment just how much the old lady loved her. 'It's not angina,' she insisted. 'More likely heartburn. I get that sometimes when I forget to eat.'

Jack didn't look entirely convinced, but Agnes looked relieved and then annoyed, as loved ones do after a fright. 'We noticed you didn't have any lunch,' Agnes said tartly. 'Next thing, you'll be getting anorexic. As if we don't have enough things to be worried about around here. Jack told me about that darned fool stallion Hilary bought. A flop, like the last one.'

'Goldplated's not a flop,' Courtney defended. 'And neither was Four-Leaf Clover. He died. That was hardly his fault. His progeny are now coming good. Lois thinks Big Brutus could win the Melbourne Cup. Do you know how much money the Melbourne Cup is worth?'

Agnes gave a scoffing laugh. 'Lord preserve us. I thought you had more sense than to believe a word that woman says when it comes to trophy races, or to start relying on horse winnings to get Crosswinds out of debt.'

'I'm not. I'm relying on Jack.'

'Well, Jack can't do miracles,' Agnes pronounced bluntly. 'I can't see any sensible investor putting his money into Crosswinds now, not with Goldplated being damned useless at his job.'

'Now, Agnes,' Jack intervened gently but firmly, his arm still around Courtney's shoulders, 'let's give the poor horse a chance. I have a hunch that the new groom Courtney hired today will bring Goldplated around to perform as required.'

'I'm pretty sure he can,' Courtney joined in. 'I was talking to him later this afternoon and he says the main problem to be avoided is setting off the bad memories the horse has in his head. So he's going to put Goldplated in a large yard with an experienced mare who's in season, and let nature takes its course without any interference from anyone. There is to be no handling at all. Sean believes a colt as young and as healthy as Goldplated won't be able to resist. He thinks that, once he gets a taste for it, he'll gradually be able to introduce some careful human handling till Goldplated won't give a hoot who's holding him, or where he's doing it.'

'Disgusting,' Agnes snorted. 'But that's the male animal for you. Still, it's not a nice topic of conversation. Do you think we could talk about something else over dinner? Speaking of dinner, I'll just go get it out of the oven. I've made the most delicious lamb hotpot, even if I say so myself. You two go and sit down. I won't be too long.'

Agnes hurried off, leaving Courtney alone with Jack on the stairs.

'Let's go,' she said straight away, feeling self-conscious at the way Jack immediately started looking her over, his eyes not missing a trick.

'You're not going out later dressed like that, are you?' he asked, an accusing edge in his voice.

'Like what?'

'Naked, under your clothes.'

'I am not naked!'

'You're damned well close to it!'

'Don't be ridiculous.'

'I'm far from being ridiculous. I'm an intelligent man. You haven't come down in that sexy gear for me. That, I know. So, who's it for, I ask? There's only one possible explanation. The new man. Sean. I saw the way he stared at you today. And I heard the way you talked about him just now. You think he's the ant's pants, don't you? You fancy him. You've arranged to meet him after dinner, haven't you? You'll make some bloody excuse about a foal when really you'll be off with that smooth-talking Irishman.'

'Now you're being *really* ridiculous,' she snapped. 'The man's old enough to be my father!'

'Still handsome, though. And fit as a fiddle, by the look of him. You like him. Why don't you admit it?'

'I like him, yes. But not in that way. He's not my type at all.'

'And what's *your* type?' he snapped.

Jack's outburst of jealousy was so typically male. Courtney had experienced male possessiveness before and after she'd had sex with a man. Yet they hadn't loved her, any more than Jack did. They'd just wanted her to be exclusively theirs till *they* decided it was time to move on.

Courtney never gave a man a chance to do that. She always sent them packing first.

Jack, of course, was a different kettle of fish. Jack, she loved. Jack, she would *never* send packing.

This frustrating realisation did not make her behave well.

'*My* type?' she threw up at him. 'I thought you were intelligent. *You're* my type, Jack. You should have no-ticed that by now. Or do you think I make a habit of crawling naked into men's beds at night? I wore these clothes for *you*, not Sean. I'm half-naked under them for *you*!''

His eyes immediately darkened, his arms snaking round her waist then yanking her hard against him. 'You little tease. Do you have any idea how much I've missed you today? How hard it's been, waiting for you to come back to the house?'

'Wonderfully hard, by the feel of things,' she taunted softly, her mouth barely centimetres away from his, their hot breaths mingling.

He sucked in sharply when she began making provocative little side to side movements with her hips.

'Stop that,' he hissed.

'Make me.'

He did, with astonishing ease, grabbing her wrists and bringing them down behind her back, lifting them upwards till she winced with the pain.

'I told you that one day someone was going to take you in hand,' he ground out through gritted teeth, an angry slash of red across his cheekbones. 'In the old days I'd have put you over my knee and paddled you till you behaved yourself. But it isn't the old days, unfortunately. Since beating you is out of the question, I'll have to use the only weapon I have: the fact you want me as much as I want you. So while you're eating your dinner think about this. Later tonight, I'm going to make love to you so much you won't be able to sit down properly for a week. There won't be a position untried, nor any foreplay forbidden. You like being on top? Be my guest. It's a great position. Leaves a man's hands free to do all sorts of things, touch all sorts of places. And there's the added bonus of being able to see every inch of your totally naked body, to watch your face twist, your eyes widen, your mouth fall open, to witness that moment when you forget where you are and who you are.'

Courtney gasped at the image of herself in such a state. And the thought of Jack, watching her.

His dark threats should have disgusted her, but they didn't. They thrilled her and excited her. Unbearably.

'For Pete's sake, where are you two?' Agnes called out from the dining room. 'Dinner's on the table!'

'Be right there, Agnes,' Jack called back, as cool as could be.

He let her wrists go, turning her and pushing her in the small of her back in the direction of the dining room. She stumbled, not because his shove was all that hard but because her legs had gone to jelly. When he reached out to steady her from behind she shrugged him away, pulling herself together and striding on ahead into the dining room. As wickedly turned on as she was, no way was she going to give Jack the satisfaction of seeing that fact.

Yes, she loved him. And, yes, she always lost her head when he was making love to her.

But she didn't have to lose her pride, or her self-respect.

Her face was as cool as his by the time she sat down at the table. She was nicely in control. Till Jack spoke.

'Did you remember to ring your accountant?' he asked.

She hadn't, of course. It had gone clear out of her mind.

'No, I didn't,' she had to confess, an embarrassed colour tingeing her cheeks. 'I forgot.'

Something close to triumph gleamed in his eyes. 'Not to worry,' he said lightly. 'You can ring him tomorrow. There's no real rush, is there? The next day will do just as well.'

'I guess so,' she mumbled, and fell to silently eating her meal.

Jack didn't try to draw her into conversation after that, a manoeuvre, she suspected, that was not out of kindness. He didn't want her to have any distraction from thinking about what he'd said out on the stairs, from thinking about that moment after Agnes had safely gone to bed and she would present herself in his room once more, not just naked this time, but already cruelly aroused.

She tried to find some will-power to fight him with, but once again the only weapon she could find against his power was a façade of boldness. She would go to him with a bang, not a whimper!

Dinner was over far too quickly, leaving several hours before Agnes's usual bedtime of ten-thirty.

If Courtney had thought the day was long, then the evening proved interminable, with Jack not letting her get away with anything. When she offered to clear up and do the washing-up, he jumped up to help her. When she settled on the sofa to watch television, he sat right beside her, instead of in the armchair he'd occupied before dinner. The only reason she didn't say she had to check on something down at the stud was because she knew Jack would come with her.

Yet she knew he wouldn't touch her. Not at that point. He would just stay with her, watching and waiting, as he was secretly watching and waiting now. She could feel it in her rapidly heating blood. He thought she'd been teasing him today, and he was paying her back in kind. And to very good effect. Inside, she was a right mess.

She didn't look a mess at ten-forty-five that night when she entered Jack's room without knocking. She was still fully dressed, for starters, which was one over Jack, who was propped up against the headboard, his chest bare against a mountain of pillows. She couldn't see the rest of him. The bedclothes were pulled up to his waist. But she suspected all of him was bare as well.

She swallowed at the thought of it, but covered her excitement with a cool smile.

'No fire tonight?' she remarked as she strolled over towards the dead hearth.

'No.' He placed his book down on the bedside table. 'I thought we would be hot enough without one.'

She arched her dark winged eyebrows and reached up to undo the gold clip in her hair. 'Did you, now?' she said, and placed it carefully on the marble mantelpiece before shaking out her hair.

'Uh-huh.'

When she turned to face him, Courtney was gratified to see tension had crept into the set of his shoulders. He looked less like a cat playing with a mouse, and more like a starving lion, desperate for a kill.

'Are you going to just stand over there all night?' he grated out.

'No.' Crossing her arms, she picked up the bottom of her black jumper and reefed it over her head in one movement, tossing it aside as though she did this sort of thing every day: stripped off before men without a qualm.

Which she possibly had, on occasion. But things were different with Jack. Everything was different with Jack. Her usual boldness was mixed with an uncharacteristic vulnerability. His hungry gaze alternately excited, then embarrassed her. Suddenly she wanted to cover herself, to not let him see her naked breasts and their rock-like nipples.

But pride had her walking brazenly towards him, her chin lifting as she tossed her curls back from her face. Unfortunately they fell forward again, as they always did when not anchored back in some way, a riotous mass of raven curls and waves which defied taming, as *she* was trying to defy taming.

'What about the rest?'

She stopped and complied, without fuss. For that would have given him all the more power.

'So what now?' she challenged once she was totally nude. 'Am I to do cartwheels? Be tied to the bedposts? What, O lord and master.' Mockery was always a good defence.

'All I want,' he growled, 'is you…in here…with me.' And he threw back the quilt.

Courtney stared at him. He was naked. And stunningly aroused.

She really should not have fallen into bed with him so eagerly, or let him plunge into her without any foreplay, or cry out his name quite so often during that first torrid mating.

But she did, and he liked it. Too much, she worried.

When he started making love to her again, she thought she acted far more restrained, until he hoisted her on top and proved to her that, with him, her being on top bore no correlation to being on top in any other way.

She tried so hard not to come, or to lose control, or to cry out his name again, but failed on all counts.

There was some comfort in Jack's lack of control as well, and the fact it was her name he cried out at his moment of release. Not Katrina's. And he didn't close his eyes once, or sigh any sad sighs.

If nothing else, Courtney could remember that fact for the rest of her life: that for one wonderful, erotic night, the man she loved thought only of her.

CHAPTER THIRTEEN

'I RANG Bill,' Courtney relayed to Jack at ten past nine the following morning. 'I told him about you, and that you wanted to see him about the stud's financial status.'

Jack was sitting at the kitchen table, having another mug of coffee after breakfast. 'And?'

'He said for us to come in straight away.'

'*Us?* I thought I'd go in alone. You said you were flat-out here. And, let's face it, I could hardly get lost. There's only the one road into Queenswood and I'm sure Mr Sinclair's office shouldn't be too hard to find. Didn't you say it was over the hardware store?'

'Yes,' Courtney admitted curtly. 'Look, it wasn't my idea we both go. It was Bill's. He sounded…odd.'

Jack put down his mug. 'In what way?'

'Stressed.'

'What's odd about that? Everybody gets stressed occasionally these days. He might have had an argument with his missus.'

'Bill doesn't have a missus. He's a crusty old bachelor. He's sixty if he's a day and married to his job and his golf clubs. No, I have an awful feeling that the bank's called in the loan.'

Jack's straight dark brows shot upwards. 'What makes you think that? Have you been getting letters of warning?'

'No.'

'Then that would be very unlikely. Still, if that *was*

the case, surely your Bill would have said something over the phone.'

'You don't know Bill. He hates relaying bad news over the phone. He prefers to do business face to face.'

'Ah…an old-fashioned gentleman, is he?'

'Yes.'

'I think I'm going to like Bill.'

This statement brought considerable irritation. Jack wouldn't be around long enough to form any real relationship with Bill. Even if his mystery client came to the party as her silent business partner, Courtney couldn't see Jack whizzing all the way up here to Queenswood on any regular basis. Face-to-face transactions were really a thing of the past, as Jack himself had just noted.

'Courtney, darling, do stop worrying,' Jack said smoothly. 'There's no point in crossing your bridges before you come to them. If your accountant has bad news, we'll deal with it together, okay?'

Courtney was taken aback, not only by the casually tossed 'darling', but his reassurance of support, no matter what. Surprise swiftly gave way to exasperation. She might be a push-over in bed where he was concerned, but she wasn't a total fool out of it!

'I don't see how,' she snapped. 'If the bank *has* called in the loan, I can't see you recommending Crosswinds as an investment at this point in time, can you? I doubt even the best sex in the world would change your mind on that score.'

'Stop jumping the gun, Courtney. Not to mention jumping to conclusions. Wait and see what Bill has to say.'

'I know what he's going to say. I can *feel* it.'

Jack rose from his chair. 'Then let's get going and see if you're right.'

Everything inside Courtney tightened. 'I'll just tell Agnes we're off.'

Bill read the letter from the bank one more time. Damn Hilary, he thought. She should have told him the bank had been sending her letters of warning. He could have advised her.

But she hadn't. She'd lied to the bank instead, saying that in November she was going to cash in a couple of large insurance policies to repay the loan. She'd even quoted company names and policy numbers. Naturally they'd hung off sending any more letters after her death, thinking those insurance policies would have definitely covered the loan, since death pay-outs were always higher than any premature pay-out figure. But a belated phone call to Hilary's named insurance company had finally shown there were no such policies.

What on earth had Hilary hoped to achieve with her lies? Time? Time for what? Winning the Lottery?

Now it was too late. The bank was closing the Queenswood branch and any pull he might have personally had with the manager there was now gone. Courtney's only hope was this investment broker she'd told him about on the phone. Jack Falconer.

But he'd have to come up with the money pretty darned quickly. The bank had only given her one miserable month to repay the loan in full, after which they were threatening to repossess and auction off Crosswinds, lock, stock and barrel. And it was no idle threat. Banks were no longer in the business of philanthropy and public relations. They played hard-ball business these days.

Bill rose wearily from behind his desk and walked over to the window to stare blankly down at Queenswood's main street, his mind wandering back to Hilary and her extraordinary behaviour. It wasn't like the woman to be such a dreamer. Or was it? Maybe her aggressive feminist manner had all been a façade. Maybe, underneath the toughness, she'd been the biggest dreamer of all.

The sight of a red convertible sports car zapping into a central parking spot directly in his line of vision snapped Bill out of his musings, his eyes widening when he finally recognised Courtney as the female passenger who climbed out.

Okay, so she was still wearing jeans. But there was no checked shirt. No dusty hat. And no unflattering ponytail. Her glorious hair was down and she was wearing a fluffy figure-hugging cream jumper with a softly rolled collar.

Never in all the years had he seen the girl looking so utterly gorgeous and feminine.

Bill's surprised eyes swung to the driver, who was at that moment striding round the front of the car to join Courtney. A tall broad-shouldered man, he had short dark hair, cut army style, and an air of decisiveness in his walk which Bill immediately liked.

He suspected Courtney must like him too, to have bothered with her appearance. Never had he known it to happen before. Jack Falconer had achieved in a few short days what no local lad had in twenty-five years.

Admittedly the man was impressive, Bill conceded as he watched him take Courtney's elbow to steer her across the street. Ruggedly handsome in looks, a gallant gentleman in manner and city-sophisticated in his dress. The trendy fawn trousers and long-sleeved open-necked black shirt he was wearing with such panache were not the sort of clothes often seen around Queenswood.

Bill's mood immediately perked up. He'd thought he'd heard something in Courtney's voice when she'd been telling him about this miracle man she'd found. Now he

knew what it was. She'd fallen for him, like a ton of
bricks.

If this Jack Falconer had fallen for Courtney in return
then he would bend over backwards to get her an investor. Men in love liked nothing better than to come to the
rescue of their fair damsel when in distress.

Of course, till this moment Bill would never have described Courtney as a fair damsel in distress…

Bill watched them disappear from view under the street
awning before hurrying back to his desk and awaiting
their arrival with a little more optimism than he had a
few minutes before.

'Probably grasping at straws,' he muttered to himself
as the seconds ticked away. 'When she finds out what
Hilary and the bank have done, she'll start acting like her
usual difficult, stroppy self, and her miracle man will be
speeding back to Sydney before I can say Jack Falconer!'

She didn't. She just sat there in one of the two chairs
he'd set out for them, looking utterly defeated.

'So that's it,' she said flatly at last, her shoulders sag-
ging, her eyes dead. 'I'm done for. Crosswinds is done
for.'

'Not necessarily,' he said, and glanced over at Jack.
'Let's hear what Mr Falconer has to say. The bank calling
in the loan shouldn't change his feelings on Crosswinds
as an investment prospect.'

'You don't understand, Bill,' Courtney broke in before
the miracle man could answer for himself. 'We have this
problem with Goldplated. It'll probably take more than a
month before we know if he's going to be any good.'

'What do you mean? Anyone who knows anything
about horses knows it'll take a good couple of *years* before you know if a new stallion's any good.'

When Courtney told him what the problem was with

Goldplated, his heart sank to rock-bottom level. 'Damn and blast,' he muttered. 'That's torn it all right.'

'Might I say something now?'

It was the miracle man who'd spoken, as cool as you please.

'Of course,' Bill said politely.

'You're both right about one thing. I couldn't advise a client to invest in Crosswinds in its present circumstances. But I have an alternative solution to Courtney's problems.'

'You *have*?' Courtney exclaimed, head swivelling round, dark eyes wide.

'What?' Bill asked.

'I will repay the loan personally.'

Bill heard Courtney's sharp intake of breath, as well as his own. When this man came to the rescue, he sure did it in style. He must love Courtney a lot!

'And before you say anything,' Jack went on swiftly, slanting Courtney a stern glance, 'yes, I can afford to. I did hint to you on several occasions that I was far from broke, but you weren't listening, and in the end I decided to drop the subject. You seemed happy believing I was practically on the breadline and, to be honest, I rather enjoyed not having the matter of money enter into the picture for once.'

For a few seconds Courtney looked like a stunned mullet, but then some kind of enlightenment came over her face, an enlightenment which clearly infuriated her.

Oh-oh, Bill groaned silently. Hilary's daughter was about to look a gift-horse in the mouth!

'There never was a mystery client willing to invest in Crosswinds, was there?' Courtney threw at Jack. 'It was you all along. You, worming your way into my good books, and then into my bed!'

Bill blinked at this news. So they were lovers already? That was good news. Very good indeed. This was just a lovers' spat, then. Nothing to be concerned about.

Clearing his throat loudly, he rose from behind his desk. 'Perhaps I should leave you two alone to discuss things. I'll just pop along to the Bluegum Café for a spot of morning tea. Be back in say…fifteen minutes?' He glanced first at a fuming Courtney and then at a splendidly composed Jack.

'Thanks, Bill,' Jack returned. 'I think that might be a wise move.'

Bill resisted smiling, for fear it would rile Courtney all the more. But the moment he was safely alone he had a good old chuckle. It seemed the girl had finally met her match!

'Now, Courtney,' Jack began calmly as soon as Bill was gone.

'Don't you "Now, Courtney" me!' she exploded, jumping to her feet and stalking across the room to the front window, where she whirled and glared at him from the safety of distance. 'You deliberately tricked me and deceived me. Lord knows what for. Do you get off playing games with other people's lives? Do you?'

'No, of course not.'

'I think you do. You've been having a great time. You yourself said how much you enjoy playing games.'

He stood up from the chair. Her hands immediately balled into fists at her sides. She was so angry she could hardly see straight. Finally she crossed her arms, because if he came near her at this moment she'd be tempted to deck him one.

'Courtney,' he said as he started walking towards her. 'There are games and there are games. Yes, I have been having a great time. I admit it. But I don't think paying off a three-million-dollar debt could qualify as a game, do you?'

His cool reasoning flustered her. 'How would I know? Maybe you get off on paying other people's debts as well! You did it before, when you didn't have to.'

His face grew serious as he reached for her, his large hands curling over her stiffly held shoulders. 'But I *did* have to,' he insisted, his eyes searching hers. 'Surely you must see that. I couldn't have lived with myself knowing all those people had lost their life savings because of my partner's greed. Just as I couldn't live with myself now if I let you and Crosswinds go under. I care about you too much for that.'

Her heart just stopped. Was he saying what she suddenly hoped he was saying. That he loved her?

'But it's not charity I'm offering you,' he continued. 'It's a deal.'

'A deal,' she repeated, dismay clutching at her heart. Not love...

A deal...

'I will clear your debts if you do something for me in return.'

'For heaven's sake, what?' It had to be something huge for three million dollars.

Jack looked worried for a second. 'This might be a bit of a shock, coming so quickly after we've met. But I'm quite sure on my part. In fact, I've never been more sure of anything.'

'Jack, for pity's sake, *what*?'

'I want you to have my child.'

Courtney was simply poleaxed.

A child. He wanted *her* to have *his* child. In her wildest dreams she would never have thought of that.

'You mean as…as some kind of surrogate?' she asked, still stunned.

'Good Lord, no. I mean we have a child together. Like any normal couple.'

The idea moved her as she would never have imagined. All her life Courtney had believed there wasn't much of the maternal in her, but the thought of having Jack's baby seemed to call not only to the woman in her but the mother.

Yet the reality of having Jack's child was fraught with more risk of future hurt than being secretly in love with him. She really shouldn't even consider it. And he shouldn't have asked her. It wasn't right.

'So what do you think?' Jack persisted when she just stood there, staring up at him.

Courtney gathered herself to answer. 'I think you have a hide,' she stated, her outer coolness a cover for her inner agitation. Because she knew that no matter what she said to him, her final answer was always going to be yes.

But she couldn't give in that easily, could she?

His smile was soft. 'Which makes us well-matched, don't you think? Any child of ours would be able to take on the world.'

Courtney's heart lurched at his words. 'I'm sorry, Jack,' she said stubbornly, 'but my answer has to be no. I would never bring an illegitimate child into this world, not after having been one myself.'

Jack shrugged. 'Marry me, then.'

The nonchalance of his proposal staggered her. Till she realised that marriage to her was just a means to an end to him. He must want a child very badly.

But he'd backed her into a clever corner with his counter-move. She'd thought her bringing marriage into things would put a spanner in the works. Instead, she was now in deeper trouble than ever.

Marry me, he'd said. Dear Lord, she'd *die* for him.

'The only reason I didn't mention marriage first,' he went on, 'was because you didn't seem the marrying kind.'

Courtney bristled, despite the accuracy of his observation. Had he been talking to Agnes about her? 'Well, I'm not,' she confessed grudgingly. 'But if there's going to be a child involved...'

'Then you will?' His hands tightened on her shoulders, his eyes lighting up with genuine delight. 'You won't regret it, Courtney. I promise you. I'll be good to you. And to our child. You won't need to worry about anything ever again. God, I—'

'I haven't said I will yet,' she broke in before he got totally carried away and took her with him. 'First, I'd like to ask you a few questions. But, before I do, do you think you could let me go?' She never could think straight when he was this close.

His hands dropped away from her shoulders and she walked back over to sit on the corner of Bill's desk, a nice distance between them. 'Right,' she began firmly, crossing her legs and clamping her hands over her top knee to stop her legs from shaking. 'I want to know when you decided to ask me this? And please don't give me any bulldust. Did you have this idea in your mind all along when you invented your mystery investor and wangled coming home with me?'

'Good Lord, no,' he denied. 'No!'

'When, then? Today...now...right here in this office?'

'Not quite. The thought did occur to me briefly the first time we made love. But I dismissed it as fanciful. I didn't think you'd agree. But today, when the idea came to me again, I felt that perhaps you would, under these new circumstances.'

'I shouldn't,' she muttered. 'It isn't right.'

'What's not right about it?'

'I'd have to be a mercenary bitch to agree to marry a man and have his baby in exchange for three million bloody dollars,' she threw at him. 'And you'd have to be a cold-blooded bastard to propose it in the first place!'

'Come now, Courtney, my offer isn't at all cold-blooded and you know it. We might not be in love with each other but we like each other one hell of a lot. The heat we generate together would put a furnace to shame. A lot of besotted couples aren't as compatible in bed as we are.'

'That's just sexual chemistry,' she argued. 'The sort which is highly unstable, I might point out. Give it six months and, poof, it will all burn out.'

'I doubt that very much.'

'Well, forgive me, but experience tells me it will. The truth is we don't know each other well enough for such a big step as marriage and a baby.'

'I know everything I need to know about *you*,' he insisted.

'In four days?' she challenged back.

'I've learnt more about you in these past four days than I knew about Katrina after four years of living with her. And I like what I've learnt. Very much so. I think you've gotten to know me pretty well, too.'

Only in the biblical sense, she thought unhappily.

Jack's frustrated sigh snapped Courtney back to the sight of him running his hands agitatedly through his hair. 'Still,' he said, an edge on his voice, 'there *are* things about me you can't possibly know, and perhaps you should. I don't want you to ever say that I tricked you or deceived you in any way. So let me put you in the total picture.'

'The total picture?' she echoed, a dark dread pooling deep inside her.

He began pacing back and forth across the room, talking and glancing over at her as he went. 'A year ago, the idea of getting married and having a child was the last thing on my mind. I thought I had everything a man could possibly want. A business which was making me millions. A house in the right part of Sydney. A glamorous lady who seemed crazy about me. A lifestyle of five-star pleasure-leisure. Then, in the space of a few months, everything changed. My partner did a flit. My business went down the tubes. I lost a fortune. Then, to top it off, my girlfriend left me for another man...'

Jack stopped his pacing to throw Courtney an uncompromisingly harsh glance. 'You believed Katrina's defection was because of money. And you know what? You could be partially right. Though that didn't occur to me at the time. I stupidly thought my still having a couple of million in the bank was enough play money for anyone. Still, the main reason Katrina left me was because I began pressuring her to have a baby.'

'You...you wanted Katrina to have your baby?' she choked out, feeling sick inside. In one fell swoop she was right back to being a stand-in for Katrina again. A second-rate substitute.

'Yes, I did,' he grated out. 'More fool me.' He shuddered at the memory, then began to pace the room once more. 'The disaster with my business partner changed me in more ways than you can imagine. Suddenly I saw the end result of living one's life for material gain and hedonistic pursuits. I started to appreciate that the simple family life my older brother led held much more satisfaction and real pleasure than my own so-called high life. I started hating the emptiness of it all. I wanted more. So I asked Katrina to marry me…and have a baby…' His pacing slowed to a halt, as did his voice.

Suddenly, his eyes were a million miles away. Such bleak, bleak eyes.

Courtney couldn't bear to think about what he was thinking about. '*And*?' she prompted harshly.

His head snapped round to her, his eyes still holding a cloud of remembered pain. 'She told me she loved me but had no intention of ever having children. She said she hated the thought of having babies. She wanted us to go on as we'd been doing, having no responsibilities except for each other's pleasure.'

Courtney didn't want to think about how well Katrina had given Jack pleasure, given he still wasn't over her.

'I told Katrina that if she wasn't prepared to settle down and have a baby, then we were through.'

Courtney was taken aback. 'You mean it was you who left her, not the other way around?'

'No. No, I have to confess that's not how it was. I arrogantly thought that, if she loved me, she'd give in to my demands. My ultimatum was a bluff. A dangerous one, considering Katrina's antagonism towards being forced to do anything at all. As you know,' he finished bitterly, 'she left me for Axelrod whom she subsequently married.'

Courtney could find no words to say at this juncture. Jack stared down at his feet for a few seconds before looking up again, his face grim.

'I won't deny I was devastated for a long time. I won't deny I came to the races last Saturday simply to see her again. Did I want her back? You may well ask. In all honesty, I don't know. I told myself I just wanted her to see that I'd survived, that I was as rich as ever. Richer, even. Yes, it's true. After Katrina left me, I began playing the stock market like some kind of self-destructive maniac, recklessly taking chances which would have given a wise investor nightmares. Perversely, I could do no wrong, and soon I had more money than before the fiasco with Graham.'

'I think you wanted to get her back, Jack,' Courtney stated, forcing *him* to face the whole rotten truth of his feelings for that woman. 'You still love her.'

'No,' he denied. 'No, I don't believe I do. Not any longer. The moment I met you, Courtney, the moment I started seeing Katrina through your very clear eyes, I knew I wanted nothing more to do with her. I also knew I wanted to get away from Sydney for a while. City life had begun to pall on me. Which is why I came up with the mystery client idea. I didn't deliberately deceive you. I was genuinely going to invest in Crosswinds if it looked like a going concern. I delayed revealing my identity so that I could spend more time with you as the man you thought I was, the not-so-successful Jack Falconer. It soothed my world-weary soul, and my badly bruised ego, to have you like me for myself. To *want* me for myself.

'You did want me for myself, didn't you?' he said softly, and began walking towards her, his eyes purposeful.

Panic had her sliding off the corner of the desk, her hands flying up to ward him off. But *his* hands were already reaching to cradle her face and his mouth was descending. Her palms ended up pressed flat against the hard wall of his chest, right above his heart.

Its thundering beat proved even more seductive than his kiss, for it showed Courtney that he wanted her for herself as well. He might still be in love with Katrina, but once *they* started making love, Courtney believed all thought of the dreaded Katrina was quickly banished from Jack's mind. If nothing else, he was hers when he was in her arms. Such thinking had her hands sliding up around his neck to pull him close. He groaned and kissed her even more hungrily, his lips prying hers apart, his tongue darting deep.

Courtney moaned, 'Oh, Jack…Jack, my darling…'

Bill's repeated clearing of his throat finally got through to the kissing couple. He wasn't surprised to find them in a torrid embrace when he returned. What did surprise him, however, was the way Courtney blushed once she saw him standing there.

To give her credit, she did her best to rustle up the girl of old.

'Fifteen minutes up already, is it?' she tossed his way as he walked over to his desk.

A sham, that boldness of hers, Bill decided. Just as Hilary's manner had been a sham. Underneath the surface aggression they were as soft and feminine as any other woman. At least, they were once the right man came along.

Bill sat down and beamed approvingly up at Jack. 'I take it you sorted things out between you?' he enquired.

'Perfectly,' Jack answered. 'If you give me the correspondence from the bank, I'll settle Courtney's loan this week.'

'Wonderful,' Bill said with genuine delight. 'And is this to be a loan on your part, or a gift?'

'A gift. You might as well know, Bill, since you're as much a family friend as an accountant. I've asked Courtney to marry me and she's said yes. That was a yes just now, darling, wasn't it?' he asked, an arm snaking possessively around her waist.

For one awful moment Bill thought she was going to say no. She'd stopped blushing somewhere along the line and he was sure he spotted a decidedly mutinous glint in her eye.

'Darling?' Jack prompted, giving her a squeeze.

She flashed him a somewhat brittle smile. 'Yes,' she confirmed, if a tad tautly.

Bill almost sighed his relief. 'Wonderful,' he said again. 'When?'

'As soon as it can be arranged,' Jack said, and Bill tried not to look shocked. What was the rush? Courtney could hardly be pregnant given she'd only met the man at the weekend.

Okay, so it was obvious they couldn't keep their hands off each other, but, given the brevity of their relationship and the fact they were already lovers, Bill would have thought it only sensible to have a longer engagement.

'And how soon would that be?' he asked Jack.

'Unless you get a special licence, you have to wait a month after you've lodged the appropriate form. So as soon as possible after that month is up. I thought a simple ceremony at Crosswinds, with a celebrant.'

Bill waited for Courtney to make some objection to Jack's plans, but she didn't. She just stood there, silent, but far from happy.

It suddenly came to Bill that maybe she hadn't fallen for Jack at all. Maybe she was just pretending. Maybe she was marrying this man for his money.

The thought shocked him. Courtney was capable of a lot of things but he hadn't thought deliberate deception was one of them. He frowned at her, and her chin shot up, her eyes suddenly as rebellious as ever.

'You've got some problem with that, Bill?' she said sharply.

'No. Not if you haven't. What about the other money you were going to ask for to bring Crosswinds up to scratch?'

'As Courtney's husband,' Jack inserted smoothly, 'I'll be only too happy to pay for any repairs and improvements necessary around our home.'

Bill saw Courtney stiffen, then throw Jack one of her blistering glances. 'What do you mean...*our* home?'

A lesser man might have wilted. But not this man. He stayed cool and composed under the fire of her eyes. 'I aim to live at Crosswinds with you, darling. We can hardly conduct a proper marriage with me in Sydney and you up here, can we?'

'I hadn't thought that far yet,' she replied tautly.

'We'll talk about it on the drive home.'

'Yes,' she bit out, 'we certainly will. Give Jack those letters he wants, Bill. We have to get going. Goldplated is having his first dry run today and I want to be there to see what happens.'

Bill did as ordered and watched with definite misgivings as Jack steered Courtney towards the door.

'Courtney,' he called out, partly in concern and partly out of curiosity.

She stopped and turned. 'Yes?'

'Could you spare me a moment, please? In private?'

'I'll wait for you in the car, darling,' Jack replied diplomatically before continuing out through the door.

'What is it, Bill?' she asked impatiently.

He waited till he was sure Jack was out of earshot.

'I hope what I'm thinking isn't true, Courtney Cross. I hope you're not marrying Jack just for his money.'

The minx laughed. 'Good God, Bill, how can you

sound so appalled when marrying a man for his money was your own idea, voiced in this office only last week?'

'But I didn't really mean it! Hilary would turn in her grave if she thought you'd do a thing like that.'

'You're wrong, Bill. Mum would probably applaud my boldness and daring. But please…do put your very decent mind at rest. I'm not marrying Jack *just* for his money.'

Bill could not contain his relief. He sighed expansively. 'Ah…so it *is* love. That was my first thought when I saw you two kissing. I said to myself, Bill, now there's a couple who are madly in love.'

Her laughter really shocked him this time. 'Heavens, you old romantic, you. Jack doesn't love me. He's still besotted with his ex, who upped and married another man. He wants me; that's all. I told you the only reason I'd ever marry a man and that hasn't changed.'

Sex? She was marrying him for the *sex*?

'The money is just an added bonus. See you at the wedding, Bill. And er…do keep this under your hat. No telling Agnes, especially. As much as Jack knows the score, I think he'd prefer everyone to think ours is the love-match of the century. I mean…it's a matter of male ego, isn't it?'

CHAPTER FOURTEEN

'WHAT did Bill want? Or shouldn't I ask?'

They had just left Queenswood, with Courtney still fuming over Jack's high-handed attitude in Bill's office. How dared he casually announce when and how they were getting married, not to mention where he was going to live, all without so much as consulting her? If this was the way he was going to act with her all the time once they were married, then he could think again. And if he thought she was going to come cap in hand for money all the time, then he could *really* think again. The man needed sorting out!

'He wanted to know if I was marrying you for your money,' she announced baldly.

'And what did you say?'

'I told him exactly what I told him last week when he himself made that suggestion.'

'*Bill* suggested you marry for money?' Jack's tone was disbelieving.

'Indeed he did. But I told him I'd never do that. I said the only reason I'd do something as stupid as marry a man was for the sex.'

Jack's amused laughter did not quell her rising temper.

'You don't believe me?' she said archly.

'I might...under other circumstances. Much as I might like to, I'm not going to fool myself into thinking my money didn't have a bearing on your saying yes...to *both* my proposals. But I'm happy that you liked me and fancied me *before* you knew I was filthy rich.'

'Just how filthy rich are you, exactly?'

'I'm no billionaire. But I'm worth a good ten million or so. Which reminds me, the day you marry me I'll have two million dollars transferred into your bank account for you to do all those things you want to do to Crosswinds. You don't have to answer to me. Spend it as you please.'

Jack's offer really took the wind out of Courtney's sails, and the heat out of her anger.

'That...that's very generous of you. But I don't really need that much. I mean I...I...'

'Of course you do,' he insisted. 'Crosswinds needs more than a coat of paint. It needs a complete update.'

'I don't know what to say.'

'I'll let you thank me tonight,' he said, slanting her a saucy smile.

The penny dropped. The extra million was a bribe to make sure she didn't change her mind about everything, and to keep her sweet in bed. Little did Jack know, but nothing short of Katrina getting him back would stop her marrying him. As for keeping her sweet in the lovemaking department...no amount of money could make her any sweeter.

In a way, she'd told Bill the truth. It was the lovemaking, rather than love, that had made her accept Jack's proposal of marriage. She could live without Jack's love. She had to. But she couldn't live without his lovemaking if she didn't have to.

And, as his wife, she wouldn't have to.

'I'm going to have to go back to Sydney tomorrow and attend to the business side of things,' Jack said. 'While I'm there I'll put in the form for a marriage licence, so you'd better give me your birth certificate before I go. I'll be back by the weekend, and this time I'll bring all my things with me.'

'You're really meaning to stay?' she asked. 'Permanently?'

'You have some objection to that?'

'No. But what are you going to do with your spare time? I mean...Crosswinds has only one boss, and that's me, Jack. I told you, I won't tolerate any interference in the running of the stud.'

'Don't worry. I won't interfere. What the hell do I know about horses, anyway? During the day I'll keep on doing what I've been doing ever since I wound up my consultancy business. I'll set myself up to trade on the stock market on the internet. Do you have a room I could use as an office?'

'You can use Mum's old study.'

'Great. That's all settled, then,' he said happily.

Courtney wasn't so sure. Life in the country was not the same as in the city. It was very quiet. And remote. There were no five-star restaurants within easy driving distance. No theatres or international sporting events. No fancy shops or galleries or wherever it was Jack had used to go with Katrina. He said he didn't want any of that any more, but old habits died hard.

'You'll get bored,' she told him.

'With you? Never!'

With me, she thought ruefully. With horses. And flies. And the heat. With everything, long before any baby arrives. Six months, she reckoned. Six months and he'd be climbing the walls. Or, worse, interfering. She would put money on it.

A silence fell in the car which didn't lift till they reached Crosswinds and were driving up towards the house.

'What are we going to tell Agnes?' she asked abruptly.

'What would you like to tell her?'

'Not the bald truth. And nothing about the baby business. You can admit you were the mystery investor all along but, after we fell in love, you decided on a different type of partnership. You can say you proposed to me on the way in the car this morning and I accepted. I don't want her knowing about the bank calling in the loan. I want her to think this is a true love-match. I'll give Bill a ring and make sure he backs me up in this.'

'Fine. But do you think she'll believe such a story? She knows you well, Courtney, and I gathered during our conversations about you that she had doubts about you ever marrying. Like mother, like daughter.'

Agnes might have thought that once, but she was not a stupid woman, and had twigged to something when Courtney came down to breakfast today wearing the jumper Sarah had given her last birthday. At the time, Courtney had confided to Agnes it was the sort of garment she wouldn't be seen dead in and was only fit for mushy girls in love. Agnes hadn't said anything when she'd spotted her wearing it, but the knowingness in her eyes had said it all. So had the barely hidden delight.

Courtney wasn't blind. Agnes thought Jack was the ant's pants. When he announced their engagement, Agnes would probably be over the moon.

She was. Utterly.

'Oh, my goodness!' she exclaimed, all of a flutter for once. 'Oh, heavens. And you're going to live here, Jack? How wonderful. And what about children? Might we eventually hear the patter of little feet?' she directed Courtney's way.

Courtney had been trying hard not to think about the baby bit, plus the fact she was virtually being paid to have Jack's child. It made her feel like some kind of expensive brood mare, selected for her genes and nothing else, a feeling added to when she recalled Jack's concern the other night about her possibly having heart trouble. Clearly, such a defect would have ruled her out as the mother of his child.

This shouldn't have hurt her, but it did. Everything about this marriage was going to hurt her in the end. Any physical pleasure she might garner from their union would come at a price.

But it wasn't fair to share any of her qualms with Agnes. After all the bad things that had happened lately, the woman deserved some happiness for a change.

'Jack and I intend starting a family straight away,' Courtney said, plastering a smile on her face.

'Oh, that's marvellous,' Agnes gushed. 'And who knows? Maybe Crosswinds will have a boy at long last.'

'You'd like a boy?' Jack asked later as they walked together down towards Goldplated's yard. Agnes had not let them go for ages, plying them with sandwiches and tea whilst asking about their plans for the wedding.

Naturally Agnes had made no objection to Jack's plans, as Courtney hadn't. There again, he'd made it all sound so romantic this time, even the getting married so quickly, especially here, on the property. Agnes had gone gaga over the idea and was already planning the wedding cake.

'Not particularly,' she replied. 'That was my mother's bent. Would you?'

'No. I don't care either way.'

'Are you going to invite your family to the wedding?'

'I don't think so. There's only my father and my brother and they both live in South Australia. Why? Did you want me to?'

'No, I guess not. Best we keep it small.'

'Who are you going to ask to give you away?'

The reality of having neither father nor mother at her wedding depressed her. 'I don't know,' she muttered. 'Does it matter?'

'You could ask Bill.'

'Yes, I could.' Which reminded her. She had to ring Bill later and clue him up on things. She could ask him then. 'Walk faster or we'll miss the mating. Sean said he'd be putting the mare in with Goldplated straight after lunch.' She hastened her step, Jack lengthening his stride to keep up with her with ease.

The yard Goldplated was stabled in was very spacious, used to agist stallions during the off season. It had a large lock-up stable in one corner and shady trees in two others. The ground was covered with good pasture, the lush green grass only worn out along the fences where the horses liked to run up and down. When Courtney and Jack arrived, both Ned and Sean were hiding behind the stable, surreptitiously watching proceedings. When she and Jack approached the fence just a few metres away from them, Sean put his fingers to his mouth in a shushing gesture.

'I just put the mare in with him. He immediately looked around to see where any people were so we skedaddled back here. Try to keep out of his direct line of vision.'

Courtney moved along the fence slightly till the stable blocked them from the horse's view. Jack moved with her, standing just behind her, his arms encircling her in what was really a very intimate and possessive position. Both Ned and Sean exchanged a knowing glance but Courtney decided not to make a fuss. They had to know how the land lay between her and Jack sooner or later, and she'd rather they too think her marriage was a love-match.

'Where did you get the mare from, by the way?' Courtney called over quietly, her stomach churning with nerves now that the moment of truth was at hand. She wanted Goldplated to perform quite desperately. It was no longer a matter of money, given Jack had come to the party, but a matter of pride. And justice. She wanted to stick one right up the ear of that person who'd done the dirty on Goldplated—and her mother—in the first place.

'Ned rustled her up from a neighbour. She's just a stockhorse. She's had five foals, and her owner says when she's in heat she's a right little tramp.'

'Good,' Courtney said. 'The trampier the better.'

'I just love the way you talk,' Jack whispered in her ear.

Courtney glanced up at him over her shoulder. 'This is business, Jack, not pleasure.'

'Yeah, right,' he said, smiling back at her.

'You'll see for yourself shortly. If we're lucky…'

The four of them fell silent whilst they watched. Initially, Goldplated was hesitant, and agitated. He wouldn't even go near the mare.

But she wasn't having any of that, the little flirt. She sidled over to him, sniffing him, then angling herself so that he could sniff her.

Goldplated must have got a good whiff of her hormone-laden scent, for, suddenly, he reared up and whinnied. Not in fear or panic, but in excitement, if the immediate state of his mating equipment was anything to go by.

'Good God,' Jack gasped.

'Shh,' Courtney reprimanded, but she too had been startled. Goldplated was obviously not one of those racehorses suffering from steroid overload. He was prime breeding material. A stud, in the most basic meaning of the word.

The mare took off, cantering around the yard, playing the tease to perfection. Goldplated was after her like a shot, giving her a tender love nip here and there, nuzzling into her neck when he could get close enough. And didn't she adore the whole ritual? Shaking her head and mane, then kicking up her heels and running off some more before finally letting herself be caught in the one empty corner. There, she backed away at first, acting like a reluctant virgin. But when Goldplated looked hesitant once more, the mare suddenly whipped around and backed up towards him, her tail swished to one side with tantalising frankness.

All right, big boy, her body language screamed. *I give in. Take me. I'm yours.*

Goldplated reared up on his hind legs and neighed his agreement.

Then, take her, he did.

For the first time in her life Courtney's mouth went dry as she watched a mating between horses. She could not take her eyes off Goldplated as he mounted the mare. The mare neighed once, then just stood there, trembling, the stallion keeping her captive with his front legs whilst his seed pumped deep into her body. It was obvious she was in a state of bliss, her flanks quivering, her back arching a little. No one witnessing such an incredibly primitive but pleasure-chocked display could doubt that a foal would result from this union, or that Goldplated would eventually get to learn to like his allotted career.

Meanwhile, Courtney had to endure the fact that Jack was pressed up against her behind with a quite stunning erection of his own. By the time the horses parted company Courtney's whole body felt stretched as tight as a drum. My God, she'd never been so turned on in her life! If only she could do what that mare had done, back up to Jack right here and now and whisper, 'Take me, I'm yours.'

But they weren't animals. They were human beings, constricted by standards of decency and decorum. They couldn't mate with no thought of where they were or who was watching. It just wasn't done.

With a struggle, she ignored her cripplingly aroused state and got on with her job as boss of Crosswinds.

'That looks promising,' she called over to Sean and Ned. 'What's your next move?'

'Ned's going to find him another experienced mare for next week,' Sean answered. 'I don't think we should overtax him to begin with. Best he wait a while. He'll be more eager that way. Then another couple of mares the following week, but with some handling involved. By then, hopefully, he should be ready to service some of your own mares.'

'That sounds great. Keep me posted.'

'Will do.'

'Come along, Jack,' she said, pushing him back from her with a brisk turn of her shoulder. 'We have work to do. A study to clean out and a birth certificate to find. Lord knows where Mum's put it. But it'll be in there somewhere.'

She was off, almost at a trot, Jack having to stride out to keep up.

'I don't want to go up to the house,' he said. 'Take me somewhere we can be alone. Right now.'

She ground to a halt and stared at him, heat zooming into her cheeks. Because she knew exactly what he had in mind. She could see it in his eyes.

'The far feed shed,' she said before she could stop herself.

'Come on, then.' He grabbed her nearest hand, began pulling her along the path.

'Not that way,' she choked out. 'This way…'

It only took them ten minutes, walking fast. Ten long, excruciating minutes.

The far feed shed had once been a grand old barn, but was now just a ramshackle building used to house straw and feed for the horses in the far grazing paddocks. With good grass in the pastures and fresh straw only being put into stables on a Monday the odds of anyone coming in there that afternoon were remote.

But it was possible.

When she told Jack this, he said he didn't give a damn and to just get her damned clothes off. *All* of them.

Did that add to her excitement, knowing someone might walk in on them?

Courtney didn't know. All she knew was she would have done anything he asked. She *did* do anything he asked. She took off every stitch she had on then bent over two bales of straw and let him take her as Goldplated had taken the mare, let him bite her on the neck, let him pump his unprotected seed in her.

It was over almost before it began, both of them climaxing together, Jack collapsing across her back, gasping. She lay underneath his heavy, heaving chest and slowly, very slowly, got her mind back.

'Jack,' she whispered at long last. 'You didn't use anything.'

He was, by this time, lying very still on top of her. Possibly exhausted, Courtney imagined.

'No,' came his rather cool reply. 'I didn't.'

A frisson of shock ripped down her spine at the

thought this omission had been deliberate, not the result of an uncontrollable passion.

'Does it matter?' he muttered. 'You did say you wanted to start a baby straight away.'

'You know I meant straight after the wedding,' she protested, panic in her voice at the realisation his timing couldn't have been better, if it had been his intention to impregnate her.

'I don't see what difference one month makes,' he said drily. 'Unless, of course, you're planning on changing your mind after you get my money.'

'You know I wouldn't do that.'

'No, Courtney. No, I don't know that, given this adverse reaction of yours to what was really a mutual recklessness. But it's good to hear you say it.'

He levered himself off her back, but when she went to rise up as well she realised he was still inside her. Not only inside, but not totally deflated. 'No, don't get up,' he said, his voice thick. 'I haven't finished yet.'

He pushed her back down with strong hands, then kept her there by massaging her shoulders and spine, swiftly bringing her back to a sensual awareness of her own not quite sated body. Her arms, which had been hanging limply down beside the bales of straw, lifted to fold and make a nest for her head. She just lay there, an odd mixture of relaxation and regathering tension. She could feel him expanding inside her but he remained still, only his hands moving, those clever, clever hands, caressing and stroking and exploring every intimate inch of her. When she began to moan and arch her back, those knowing hands grabbed her hips and lifted her up onto her knees.

'You do it,' he urged, and showed her what he wanted.

She groaned, but obeyed, rocking back and forth, making love to him with her body, her head still down on her forearms, her eyes squeezed tightly shut. If someone had walked in on them then she wouldn't have seen them, or cared. She was in another world, a world where nothing existed but what she was doing. She begged him to move also. But he didn't. Not till she was beside herself, till she was sobbing with frustration. Then and only then did he move, his knowing hands joining in once more, stroking her aching breasts before sliding down her stomach between her legs, touching that magical spot which shattered her apart.

She cried out his name, then just cried.

Oh, Jack…Jack…what have you done to me?

CHAPTER FIFTEEN

COURTNEY hung up the phone and walked disconsolately back into the kitchen. 'Jack's not coming back till Sunday, now,' she said drearily. 'He said it took him a lot longer to do everything than he realised. He also said he's got far too much stuff to fit into his car, so he's asked Lois to bring up the rest. She's coming up on Sunday as well, to pick up that horse, remember?'

Agnes glanced round from where she was standing at the sink, washing up. 'The one you've been trying to skinny up?'

'Yep. That one. You know, Jack must have one heck of a lot of clothes if he can't fit them in his car. Lord knows where he'll ever wear them all.'

Agnes pulled the plug in the sink. 'I don't think it's all clothes. He promised to buy me a dishwasher while he was down in Sydney. And he said something about a computer for Sarah.'

Courtney frowned. 'He never said anything to me about any of that.'

'He wanted it to be a surprise. I'm only telling you now to put your mind at rest. I'm pretty sure he's planning on buying you something special too, so you can stop pouting.'

'I'm not pouting.'

'Oh, yes, you are. You've been in a bad mood ever since Jack left.'

'I have not.'

'You can't fool me. You miss the man. And why shouldn't you? You're in love.'

'I don't think I like being in love,' she muttered.

'Yes, I gathered that too. But you'll get used to it, in time. Jack's a good man. You'll be happy with him, if you let yourself be. But if you start carrying on like your mother did with men you'll make yourself miserable.'

'I'm *not* like my mother!'

'You are in some ways.'

Courtney bristled. 'Truly, whose side are you on?'

'Does there have to be sides?'

'There are always sides where men and women are concerned.'

'Who said so? Hilary?'

'No, *me*. They always want the upper hand.'

Agnes shrugged. 'I don't think Jack's like that at all. He's a nice man. Kind and helpful. You should thank your lucky stars for the day he fell in love with you, because not many men would.'

'Well, thank you very much!'

Agnes shot her an uncompromising look. 'I only have your best interests at heart, girl. I'm worried you're going to do something to ruin this. Jack is the best thing that's ever happened to you, and to Crosswinds. So be careful. And behave!'

Courtney only just resisted throwing at Agnes exactly what sort of man Jack was. An opportunist, that was what. A man with a ruthless agenda. A man possibly driven by vengeance against a woman he was still besotted with.

He doesn't love me, she wanted to scream. *He's just using me. I'm no better than a brood mare, all paid for and properly serviced, according to plan. The bottom line is that only the baby matters to him. Not me. Not our marriage. They're totally irrelevant. He'll divorce me as good as look at me once I've had his precious child!*

This last thought brought Courtney up with a jolt. Actually, all her thoughts had jolted her. She hadn't realised they'd been lurking somewhere in her head.

Not that they changed anything. Even knowing the worst, she still wanted Jack, wanted him so badly that the wait till Sunday seemed an eternity. Yet it was only two days away. Two never-ending, miserably lonely days.

Everything inside Courtney seemed to tighten, then shatter. No wonder her mother had warned her about this kind of thing happening. It was hell. It was agony. It was unendurable!

'I'm going for a ride,' she announced abruptly.

Courtney reined the big bay gelding to a halt at the top of the highest hill on Crosswinds, a spot where the whole property was laid out before her. Her troubled eyes travelled slowly over all she owned, but, try as she might she couldn't muster up the passion she'd once had for it. All she could think about was Jack.

This was Sunday, the third day in a row she had ridden up here and just sat on her horse, thinking about him. They were terribly mixed up thoughts. One moment she clung to the hope that he did care for her, that he was done with Katrina once and for all and was genuine in his desire to embrace family life here at Crosswinds. Then, the next moment, doubts would crowd back in, fuelled by several recent incidents. First Jack's delaying his return. Then his vagueness over *exactly* what was taking him so long down there. Finally his taking an age to answer the phone last night, then sounding distracted when he did.

This morning her doubts far outweighed her hopes, due to an article in the Sunday paper that the minister for sport and his beautiful wife, Katrina, had parted company during the week and would be seeking a divorce. The article reported that Mr Axelrod had been tight-lipped about the split but it was rumoured there *was* a third party involved. Mrs Axelrod admitted she had left her husband's harbourside mansion and was currently staying with an old friend somewhere in Sydney.

The idea that Katrina was staying with Jack had taken hold on reading this, and simply wouldn't let go.

What would she do if Jack rang her today and said he wasn't coming back after all?

The sudden sighting of dust in the distance brought her bolt upright in the saddle, her neck craning, her heart pounding. *Yes!* It was coming from the road to Queenswood. A vehicle, speeding towards Crosswinds.

Yet Jack wasn't due for a couple of hours. Not unless he'd started with the dawn. Maybe it was Lois. She was known to get on the road very early.

The sun burst out from behind the clouds and Courtney spotted flashes of red between the trees lining the road. Red! It was a red car. It was Jack, hurrying back to her.

Courtney sobbed with relief, then kicked her mount into an instant gallop, tearing down the hill and across the paddocks, jumping any fences in her way. She vowed not to think such negative thoughts any more, or to worry that Jack didn't love her. He liked her. He desired her. And he'd come back to her. That would do for now.

She sailed over the last fence, which brought her onto the winding gravel driveway just as Jack drove through the main gate. He braked to a halt barely metres from the horse's dancing front feet, his handsome face darkening with instant fright. And a measure of fury.

'Courtney! Are you stark raving mad, jumping fences like that? What if you'd fallen?'

She grinned down at him, finding immense satisfaction in his angry concern. 'It wouldn't be the first time. You don't need to worry about me.' But it was nice that he did.

'But what if you're pregnant?'

All the pleasure in his return drained out of her. 'And if I am, am I to stop riding altogether?' she threw at him. 'Is my life going to come to a halt simply because I'm carrying Jack Falconer's child?'

'I would expect you to be sensible,' he ground out. 'So, yes, I'd prefer you to stop riding.'

'I'll bet you won't stop me riding *you* tonight, though,' she pointed out tartly. 'After all, I might *not* be pregnant yet. And that's your main priority, isn't it? Getting me knocked up.'

'Courtney, for pity's sake...'

'Pity, Jack? What's pity got to do with any of this? This is nothing but a deal, remember? Your millions in exchange for my womb. Did you think all that great sex had scrambled my brains? Oh, no, Jack, I know exactly where I stand with you now.'

'And where's that, Courtney?' he asked through clenched teeth, his knuckles white on the steering wheel.

'Nowhere of any lasting value.'

'That's not true.'

'Our marriage will be a sham and you know it. So why bother? Keep your two million pieces of silver. I'll still have your baby, since I probably already am knocked up. But I won't be marrying you. The price is just too high.'

He glared up at her for a long moment. 'Lois isn't far behind me,' he said, making an effort to be calm despite the stubborn set of his jaw. 'So let's keep this argument till later.'

'There'll be no argument later. My mind is made up. No marriage, Jack. And that's final!'

His face tightened. 'You don't mean that.'

'I do.'

'I thought you cared about me.'

'I thought *you* cared about *me*,' she countered, tears smarting her eyes. 'But you don't. Tell me, Jack. What took you so long to answer the phone last night? Have a visitor, did you?'

And there it was. That momentary flicker in his eyes. Courtney paled. 'My God, Superbitch *was* there, wasn't she? You were in bed with her when I rang.'

'Of course I wasn't. Don't be ridiculous.'

Suspicion swiftly gave way to rage, a rage born of pain. 'Ridiculous, am I? I'll show you how ridiculous I am. I want you to turn right round and go back where you came from. Get the hell out of here and out of my life. I'll pay you back every cent, if I have to sell every damned horse I own. And let me tell you this, if I *am* having your baby, you are never going to see it. *Never!*'

Reefing on the reins, she dug her heels in and rode off even more wildly than she'd approached, uncaring of her safety, uncaring of anything. Tears streamed down her face as she jumped fence after fence, not stopping till she'd put plenty of distance between her and Jack, and only halting then because she could no longer see. She stopped she knew not where, slid down off the gelding's sweating back, then leant against him, clutching the saddle and sobbing her heart out.

'And why would a lucky lass like you be crying your eyes out like that?'

Courtney swung round, brushing her hair back from

her blotched face and blinking madly. Sean was leaning against a nearby fence, his dark eyes watching her.

Embarrassment put her immediately on the defensive. She dashed any remaining tears away with the backs of her hands, her chin lifting defiantly. 'Lucky, am I? How in hell do you figure that out?'

'You have this wonderful property. Hundreds of fantastic horses. Two very handy stallions and another who could be anything. On top of that, you'll soon be getting married to a man I hear is crazy about you.'

'Jack? *Crazy* about me?' She laughed. 'You have to be joking. All Jack cares about is himself!'

Sean looked genuinely taken aback. 'Are we talking about the same Jack here?'

'Who else?'

'Sarah said he was a real good bloke.'

'What would she know? She's as silly as Agnes. God, if only my mother was here. She'd understand. She'd be on my side. There again, Mum loved me,' she muttered.

'I love you too.'

Shock sent Courtney's eyes flinging wide. 'What? What did you say?'

'I said I love you too.'

'Are you mad? You don't even know me. Why, you're…you're old enough to be my…'

'Father?' he finished for her, smiling the strangest, saddest smile. 'That's because I am.'

'You are what?'

'Your father.'

She just stared at him, utterly speechless.

'I'm sorry,' he went on. 'I guess I shouldn't have blurted it out like that.'

All Courtney could do was stare at him, suddenly seeing the similarities between them. The eyes. The nose.

The jaw line. 'You're my father,' she said weakly. A statement of fact, not a question.

Courtney felt both dazed and confused. Where was the fury she'd always thought she would feel if her father ever *dared* show up again in her life?

He smiled softly again. 'Please don't be angry with me. I didn't desert you, you know. I always wanted to be a part of your life. But Hilary wouldn't let me. She wouldn't even let me *see* you. And you know your mother,' he added grimly. 'She could be like a brick wall.'

Courtney tried not to go to mush, because for all she knew he was lying. 'Why didn't you apply to the courts for custody rights, then?' she challenged. 'They would have granted you some as my father.'

'I had no proof, and this was before DNA tests, remember? No, that wouldn't have worked. Hilary would have fought me and it would have become ugly.'

'Well, of course Mum would have fought you. You broke her heart, don't you know that? Because of you, my mother *hated* men.'

'Hilary hated men long before I came along. It had something to do with her father rejecting her because she wasn't a lad. Look, I don't know what your mother told you about me, but I can guess. I seduced her because I had my eye on Crosswinds? I made her pregnant to trap her into marriage and get my greedy hands on her property and her horses? Am I close?'

'You left the bit out about being caught with one of the stable girls at the same time as you were sleeping with my mother.'

'Oh, lovely,' he said with a bitter twist to his mouth. 'I wasn't just a gold-digger, I was a serial seducer as well.'

'Are you saying none of this is true? That my mother lied?'

He shrugged. 'Maybe she convinced herself afterwards it was true. Maybe she thought that was the sort of man I was. Yeah, there was a stable girl. And, yeah, we were seeing each other. But that was *before* I slept with your mother. Look, I don't want to paint your mother out badly in your eyes, Courtney, but in all fairness I'd like to be telling my side of the story.'

'All right,' she said, still slightly dazed.

'Yeah, Hilary found me physically attractive, but she wasn't in love with me. She wanted an heir for Crosswinds and she paid me to sleep with her. Two thousand dollars.'

Courtney's eyes bulged.

'A pittance, you'll probably be thinking. But it was a fortune to me at the time. I was twenty-five and stony broke. The money bought me a motorbike.'

As her initial shock waned, Courtney conceded it was possible. It was the sort of thing her mother was capable of doing.

'Hilary chose me the same way she'd have picked a stallion,' Sean added bitterly. 'She told me I had all the right genes she wanted to pass on to her son. Good looking. Well-built. Nice eyes. And I was great with horses. Fearless, she said. She liked that most of all. She believed my being half-gypsy meant horses were in my blood, and my children would have that same blood. Which, I have to admit, turned out to be right. You can ride, lass. And you're fearless. Your mother got what she wanted in that, even if you did turn out to be a lass instead of a lad.'

Courtney couldn't help being fascinated by Sean's story. It was so bizarre it just had to be true. 'You're really half-gypsy?'

'Romany. On my father's side. My mother was Irish. My parents never married. I carry my mother's surname. My father used to leave her with regular monotony, only coming back when he needed a roof over his head, or some money, or some sex. My mother was besotted with him, but he was a wanderer.'

'If what you say about my conception is true,' Courtney said, 'why would you think my mother would ever let you have anything to do with raising me in the first place? You must have known she'd get rid of you once she was pregnant.'

Sean sighed. 'That was my plan too, at the start of things. I reckoned on one night and I'd soon be out of there with my two grand. But it didn't work out quite that way. Hilary was not a young woman. It took months before she fell. And by then things had changed. I fell in love with her.'

'But she was twenty years older than you!' Courtney protested. 'And hardly a beautiful woman.'

'I know that. But it was strange. After a while, I didn't notice any of that. She had a damned good body and she was very passionate. In the end, I couldn't stay away from her. When she finally told me she was expecting, I asked her to marry me.'

'My God! And what did she say?'

'She laughed, then fired me, with no references. You can imagine how I felt. I argued with her. I pleaded. I even made love to her one last time in some mad attempt to reach her. And I thought I had. She was...well, she was a wee bit upset afterwards. But then, suddenly, it was like she brought down some hard shell over her feelings. She turned on me, warning me that I had no real proof I was her baby's father, and that if I ever made any demands on her, or the child, I would regret it till my dying day. So I left, drove off on my well-earned motor bike. But not for her. For *you*,' he insisted, his dark eyes intense.

Courtney sucked in a deep breath, then let it out in a slow, shuddering sigh. Her father's eyes never left hers for a second.

'There wasn't a day that I didn't think of you,' he insisted, in a voice throbbing with emotion. 'Or wonder what you were like, what you were doing. I tried to keep an eye on you from a distance. I knew Hilary had a girl, and I knew she was a beauty. I used to hang around Queenswood, hoping for a glimpse of you. But it never happened, and in the end I had to get away. Right away. So I went to other states to work. Even then I used to hear things about Hilary Cross. She was a woman people talked about. When I found out she'd bought Goldplated, it bothered me. I didn't much care that *she'd* been cheated, but I cared for you. That horse was part of your inheritance. When I heard she'd died, I just had to come and help my little girl.'

Emotion mushroomed up from Courtney's heart like an atomic cloud, clogging her throat. 'That was very kind of you,' she managed. 'Thank you.'

'I didn't mean to tell you I was your father. I don't expect anything from you. I understand you don't know me, and couldn't possibly love me...'

Tears actually came into his eyes.

Courtney wasn't sure who made the first move, but seconds later they were in each other's arms, hugging and weeping.

'Oh, lass...lass,' he cried.

She couldn't speak. She just clung to him.

'So this is what's been going on since Jack went away. Courtney Cross, I'm ashamed of you!'

CHAPTER SIXTEEN

LOIS could hardly believe her eyes. She'd been shocked earlier this week when Jack had rung and announced he and Courtney had fallen in love and were getting married. But, once she'd got used to the idea, she'd thought they were a great match and their marriage the answer to everyone's prayers, hers included.

So she'd been doubly shocked on arriving at Crosswinds a little while ago to find that Jack was already in the process of leaving again, saying Courtney believed he'd been sleeping with Katrina while he was in Sydney and had told him to get lost, so he was going to, as soon as he'd unloaded everything.

Now she was triple-shocked to find Courtney in the arms of another man, making her accusation of Jack being unfaithful look very hypocritical indeed!

'This isn't what it looks like,' Courtney said shakily on pulling out of the stranger's close embrace.

Scepticism was Lois's first reaction once she got a good look at Courtney's bit on the side. This was a seriously sexy-looking guy, despite the fact he had to be well over forty.

'I'm not Courtney's lover, Ms Wymouth,' the sexy stranger said firmly.

Lois could not decide whether to be annoyed that he recognised her. Or flattered. 'Oh, really?'

'He's not,' Courtney insisted, her cheeks as red as her eyes. 'He's my father.'

Lois didn't usually gape. But this time she did.

'I…I didn't know till today,' Courtney went on, more flustered than Lois had ever seen her. 'Sean's been here this past week, helping us with Goldplated. You see he and Mum…they…oh, it's such a long story!'

'Too long to tell me now,' Lois said swiftly. 'In a few minutes Jack will be doing what you told him to do earlier. Are you quite sure that's what you want? Because, if it isn't, you'll have to hurry to stop him from leaving.'

Courtney stiffened. 'I don't care if he does leave. He doesn't love me. He still loves Katrina.'

'What a load of old rubbish. Jack doesn't love her. He loves you. He told me so himself.'

'He was just saying that. It's the story we agreed upon to tell everyone.'

Lois felt like slapping the silly little fool. 'You think I can't tell the difference between a made-up story and the truth? The man's crazy about you. I ought to know. I've spent the last few days being dragged from shop to shop whilst he bought you everything under the sun for your wedding. Rings. Clothes. Shoes. Lingerie. Perfume. No man goes to that much trouble for a woman he doesn't love. He told me he knows how busy you are up here at the moment and he wants everything to be absolutely perfect for you.'

'That's all very romantic-sounding, Lois,' the girl still argued, 'but nothing you've said changes anything. It's a game Jack's playing. Just a game. He's playing perfect fiancé. But he's not perfect. He was in bed with his ex-girlfriend last night. I know it.'

'He said that was what you thought, but it's not true. She was there at the house, admittedly, but she just showed up out of the blue and insisted on talking to him. He said he heard her out then sent her away again. He swears he never touched her. He said he can't stand a bar of her any more.'

'Well, he would, wouldn't he? He wants our marriage to go ahead.'

'Why would he want that, if he still loved Katrina?' Lois pointed out logically.

'Why? Because of the baby, that's why!'

'The baby!' both Lois and Sean exclaimed at once.

Sean turned Courtney to face him. 'You're having Jack's baby?'

'I...I might be. I don't know yet. But, yes...it's on the cards.'

His dark eyes blazed. 'And you're sending him *away*?'

'He...he doesn't love me, Dad,' Courtney cried. 'I can't bear it if he doesn't love me.'

'Oh daughter, daughter, don't do what your mother did. Don't send Jack away without talking things out with him. He might not love you as much as you love him, but he very well might. He might love you even more. You'll never know if you don't find out. You told me earlier your mother loved me. If she did, then she never said so. Maybe she was afraid to. Maybe she thought I was too young. Or maybe—like you with Jack—she thought I didn't love her back. If only she'd been honest with me, we might have married, or at least come to some kind of understanding, and I wouldn't have lost all those years of being your father. So for your baby's sake, if no one else's, go to your Jack and talk to him. Tell him how much you love him.'

'I...I can't,' she wailed, her face anguished.

'You *can't*? You, Courtney Cross, the most fearless lass I've ever known, *can't* tell a man she loves him? I've never heard so much balderdash in all my life. Now, get yourself up to the house before your man gets away. And don't walk. *Ride!*'

Lois was amazed at the man's strength. For someone not all that tall or that big, he hoisted Courtney up into the saddle as if she was a feather.

Great hands, Lois thought as she watched him. Great eyes. Great buns too.

I wonder if he needs a job…

Courtney's head spun as she rode towards the house, her heart pounding along with the horse's hooves. Too many emotions were see-sawing through her. Too many contradictory thoughts.

Jack doesn't love me. I know he doesn't. How could he? How could any man?

Yet Lois seemed so sure…

And then there was what Sean had just said to her.

You don't really want to end up like your mother, do you?

She kicked the horse into a faster gallop and rounded the last corner, which brought the house into view, only to see Jack climbing in behind the wheel of the red sports car.

'Jack, *wait!*' she called out. But he must have gunned the engine at that moment for he didn't hear her. With a spray of gravel, the car was off, and gone.

She took off after him, but the car was too fast for her. Way too fast.

She'd never catch him, not even if she cut across the yards. Yet she had to try, didn't she? She couldn't just give up now!

It was madness, the speed at which she started taking the fences. The horse only had to put one foot wrong and they would fall.

The thought of actually losing Jack's baby, a baby she didn't even know she'd conceived as yet, jolted her so much that she immediately reined the horse in, and just watched Jack drive away. She watched till there were no specks of red through the trees. Watched till all the dust his car kicked up had dissipated and there was nothing left to show that he'd ever been there, nothing but a child, perhaps, already growing inside her.

It was a falsely calm Courtney that returned to the house and walked slowly upstairs to her room, where she found several boxes and plastic bags dumped on her bed.

With dry eyes, she opened them one by one, then carried them into the guest room where she laid them all out on the velvet spread. The lovely white lace suit. The matching picture-hat. The pearl high heels. The luxurious and quite sexy underwear. The huge bottle of perfume. The velvet box of matching wedding rings. And, last but not least, the beautiful ruby and diamond engagement ring.

She stared at that ring for a long time before clutching it to her heart and slowly sinking to the floor by the bed, her head coming to rest against one of the posts. She didn't cry. She was beyond tears. Way, way beyond.

She heard Agnes's footsteps on the staircase, and willed her not to come in to the room.

She didn't. It was Jack who walked in. Jack who came over and lifted her up into his arms.

'Now, you listen to me,' he said, cupping her face and looking deep into her eyes. 'I love you, Courtney Cross. *You*, not Katrina. And I know you love me. So don't you ever tell me to go away again. Because I'm not going to. I'm not going to leave you ever again. We're going to be married and we're going to have babies together. And we're going to live happily ever after.'

And, with that, he folded her against his huge chest, crushing her close, his lips in her hair.

'Now tell me you love me,' he insisted. 'No waffle. No bulldust. Just say, I love you, Jack.'

'I love you, Jack,' she choked out, still clutching the ruby ring to her heart.

He sighed. 'About time, too.'

EPILOGUE

'GUESS who I just saw in the ladies',' Courtney whispered to Jack on returning to the members' stand.

'Don't tell me,' he said drily. 'Katrina.'

'Got it in one! Would you believe she didn't recognise me at first with my glad rags on?' Courtney was wearing the glorious white lace bridal suit Jack had bought her, complete with picture-hat. Lois had suggested it, saying that such an outfit wouldn't look at all out of place at the Melbourne Cup meeting.

Now that she was there, Courtney had to agree, and she did look pretty good, even if she had to say so herself. Perhaps even better than on her wedding day, her figure having filled out somewhat now that she was three months pregnant. Did she have a bust, or what!

'And?' Jack probed.

'Once she realised who I was, she gave me a panicky look, then disappeared like a shot.'

'Good to see she took heed of what I told her that night.'

Courtney glanced up at her handsome husband, who was looking simply splendid in a light grey suit. 'Which was what, exactly? I never did ask you.' It was just curiosity asking. Courtney hadn't doubted Jack's love since the day he came back for her.

'After she came out with all that drivel about realising she'd made a mistake and that she still loved me, I told her she had absolutely no idea what love was, that all she loved was her own selfish self. I warned her that if

179

she was ever to show up on my doorstep again, or ring me or try to contact me or do anything to destroy my relationship with you, then she had better emigrate. Fast! Then I told her to get her pathetic hide back to her husband, because soon her inner ugliness would show in her face and then no man would want her, not even one as stupid and shallow as George.'

'And did she? Go back to him?'

'I gather she did, which is why she's here today.'

'My God, her husband's not presenting the Melbourne Cup, is he?' As much as she wasn't undermined by Katrina any more, the less she saw of the woman, the better.

'No,' Jack confirmed.

Courtney sighed her relief. 'Not that we'll have to worry about that,' she went on. 'I mean, Lois has done wonders just getting Big Brutus into the race today. His win last week in the Werribee Cup was simply fantastic, but this race is so hard. As much as I'd be over the moon if he won, I can't seriously get my hopes up. A place would be lovely, though.'

'Mmm,' was all Jack said, and Courtney looked at him.

'You haven't put too much money on, have you, Jack?'

'What? Who, me? No, no...not all that much.'

'Mmm. Then why are you looking so worried all of a sudden?'

'I...er...well, the thing is, Courtney. I backed the darned horse each way. I hope you don't think I'm a wimp.'

She laughed. Him? A wimp? Her tower of strength? Her magnificent man? 'Don't be silly, Jack. Big Brutus is forty to one. And this is the Melbourne Cup. Everyone bets each way in the Melbourne Cup.'

'Not everyone,' he mumbled.

'What? What are you talking about?'

'Nothing. It's just that Agnes and Bill asked me to put a bet on for them both. And they didn't want it each way.'

'Yes, but they only bet small, whilst you, Jack, are a serious gambler.'

'Me?' He looked surprised.

'Yes, you. Only a serious gambler would have married someone like me.'

His eyes softened on her and Courtney smiled. She loved it when he looked at her like that. She loved everything about Jack. He was a wonderfully kind and big-spirited man and she couldn't wait till their baby was born. She rather hoped they'd have a son, but she wasn't stressing over it. A daughter would be just as welcome. Jack continued to insist he didn't mind either way, but she suspected he might like a little boy first.

A hush came over the crowd as it did in those tense moments in the Cup after the field had taken their place and the starter was on his stand, watching and waiting till the horses settled before he pressed the bell and the gates sprang open.

Surprisingly, Courtney wasn't as nervous as she'd been the week before, when she'd watched the Werribee Cup on the TV. Just getting Big Brutus into the Cup had satisfied her, and hopefully satisfied her mother, if she was up there, watching.

Courtney had felt very angry with her mother for quite a while after what Sean had told her, but it was hard to stay angry with a dead woman, especially when that woman was your mother. Besides, after all Courtney had recently been through, she realised it was impossible to judge another person's actions. Who knew what inner demons had fashioned her mother's thoughts and actions?

The roar of the crowd had her snapping back to the race. They were off!

Courtney stretched up on tiptoe and searched for Big Brutus's colours, amazed to find them not where she'd been looking, at the tail of the field, but out in front.

'My God, he's leading!' she gasped as they flashed past the post the first time.

Courtney shot a frowning glance over at Lois, who was standing on the other side of Jack, but Lois's eyes were glued on the track and she was clutching the arm of the man on the other side of her, a very handsome man in a very sexy black suit.

Courtney smiled an amused smile. Sean hadn't wanted to come to Melbourne with them. He'd had to be persuaded, both into the trip and the suit. But the moment he'd seen Lois, dressed fit to kill today, he'd been bewitched, and slightly bewildered, Courtney thought. Lois in race-day mode was a hard force to resist.

'He's gone further in front,' Jack groaned, and Courtney's eyes reefed back to the track.

He certainly had. Three lengths, in fact. Her stomach began to churn now as the butterflies of hope invaded. It wasn't impossible for a horse to lead all the way in the Cup, she reasoned. It *had* been done. And Big Brutus wasn't carrying much weight.

Still, these were daring tactics. Lois must have told the jockey to do this. He wouldn't have taken it upon his shoulders to ride such a bold race without being instructed to.

They were entering the back straight and Big Brutus went even further in front. Five…six lengths. Yet he was just loping along, his head on his chest.

Emotion welled up in Courtney's chest.

Are you watching this, Mum? This is your horse out there. You bred him. Isn't he just magnificent?

It wasn't till they swung into the straight, with Big Brutus still in front by four lengths, that the combination of hope and exhilaration overwhelmed Courtney. She started jumping up and down, screaming encouragement and instructions at the top of her lungs.

'Go, big boy, go! No, don't whip him. Just ride him. Hands and heels. You can do it, big boy. Not much further now. Yes, that's it. Stretch. Stick your neck out. Don't let them get you. Don't stop. Don't look. You can do it. This is your race. Your year. Your time. Yes, yes, *yes*!' As Big Brutus crossed the line, a gallant neck in front, Courtney threw her hands up into the air in victory.

'He did it, Jack,' she cried, turning to her husband. 'He did it!'

Jack's binoculars dropped back down onto his chest. 'My God, he did,' he rasped, looking a bit green around the gills. 'He really did.'

Courtney laughed, then hugged him.

People began tapping them on the shoulders, congratulating them. It reminded Courtney to do the same to Lois, but when she looked over at Big Brutus's trainer, Lois was otherwise occupied.

Jack's pressing what looked like betting tickets into her hand turned her attention away from her trainer kissing her father.

'What's this?' she asked.

'I found them in a secret drawer in your mother's desk.'

Courtney stared down at the tickets. Each was on Big Brutus to win the Melbourne Cup, placed months before, when Hilary had first entered the horse. Each was for thousands and thousands of dollars, and not for much outlay, either, since his price then had been huge.

'Your mother's insurance policies,' Jack said.

Courtney glanced up. A great big lump on her throat. 'Oh, Jack...'

He nodded. 'I didn't want to tell you, in case the horse lost.'

'You were protecting me,' she said, continually in awe of the many ways Jack showed her his love.

'I didn't want you to think your mother a total fool.' He inclined his head in the direction of where Sean and Lois were still glued together. 'You can't blame her, you know, for not trusting your dad. He was way too young. And way too good-looking. She did what she thought she had to do to survive, Courtney.'

'Yes,' she said, nodding. 'Yes, you're right.'

'Their romance was nothing like ours. We're well matched, you and I. True equals. True partners.'

Courtney knew what he meant. Now that she was secure in Jack's love, she wanted to share everything with him, even Crosswinds. She no longer saw his help as interference. Though he still had absolutely no horse sense.

But he was very smart with money.

'I was thinking, Jack, now that Goldplated's come good and I have all this spare cash, do you think you might like to become Crosswinds' financial manager? I mean...the stud's going to get pretty busy in the coming years, and I'm not going to have as much time once I become a mum.'

He just looked at her. And then he smiled.

'You are a wonderful woman, Courtney Falconer.'

'Yes, I agree. But will you?'

He grinned. 'I'd love to.'

Lois finally descended upon them, looking flushed and excited. 'That was simply fantastic, wasn't it?'

'Fantastic,' Courtney returned, not sure if Lois meant the race, or the kiss. 'And so are you, Lois.'

'Oh, no. Big Brutus deserves all the praise. And your mum. She bred him. Shall we go lead him in together?'

'I think the press might grab you first,' Courtney warned.

'Mmm, yes, they probably will. Do I look all right?'

'You look absolutely beautiful,' Sean said by her side, and Lois beamed up at him.

Courtney and Jack exchanged looks, their eyes dancing with knowing amusement.

'Guess who's not going to go to bed alone tonight?' Jack whispered in Courtney's ear as they pushed their way through the crowd.

'Golly. Who?'

'You, you sexy thing.'

Courtney's eighteen-week ultrasound showed she was having a boy. Nicholas Preston Falconer was born five days late on the seventh of May, weighing nine pounds five ounces. Agnes delivered him, with Jack her willing but slightly anxious helper. Sean and Lois were married the same day the baby was christened.

If you enjoyed what you just read,
then we've got an offer you can't resist!

Take 2 bestselling love stories FREE!

Plus get a FREE surprise gift!

Clip this page and mail it to Harlequin Reader Service®

IN U.S.A.	IN CANADA
3010 Walden Ave.	P.O. Box 609
P.O. Box 1867	Fort Erie, Ontario
Buffalo, N.Y. 14240-1867	L2A 5X3

YES! Please send me 2 free Harlequin Presents® novels and my free surprise gift. Then send me 6 brand-new novels every month, which I will receive months before they're available in stores. In the U.S.A., bill me at the bargain price of $3.34 plus 25¢ delivery per book and applicable sales tax, if any*. In Canada, bill me at the bargain price of $3.74 plus 25¢ delivery per book and applicable taxes**. That's the complete price and a savings of at least 10% off the cover prices—what a great deal! I understand that accepting the 2 free books and gift places me under no obligation ever to buy any books. I can always return a shipment and cancel at any time. Even if I never buy another book from Harlequin, the 2 free books and gift are mine to keep forever. So why not take us up on our invitation. You'll be glad you did!

106 HEN C22Q
306 HEN C22R

Name _____ (PLEASE PRINT)

Address _____ Apt.#

City _____ State/Prov. _____ Zip/Postal Code

* Terms and prices subject to change without notice. Sales tax applicable in N.Y.
** Canadian residents will be charged applicable provincial taxes and GST.
All orders subject to approval. Offer limited to one per household.
® are registered trademarks of Harlequin Enterprises Limited.

PRES00 ©1998 Harlequin Enterprises Limited

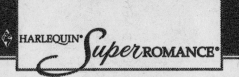